TOM ANGLEBERGER

AMULET BOOKS
LONDON

DARTH PAPER
STRIKES BACK

AN oRIGAMI YoDA BooK

ISBN: 978-1-4197-0127-6

Printed and bound in U.S.A.
10 9 8 7 6 5 4 3 2

Amulet Books are available at special discounts when purchased in quantity for premiums and promotions as well as fundraising or educational use. Special editions can also be created to specification. For details, contact specialsales@abramsbooks.com or the address below.

ABRAMS
THE ART OF BOOKS SINCE 1949

The Market Building
72-82 Rosebery Avenue
London, UK EC1R 4RW
www.abramsbooks.co.uk

THIS BOOK IS DEDICATED TO
SUSAN VAN METRE,
WHO BELIEVED IN ORIGAMI YODA
FROM THE BEGINNING.

DARTH PAPER STRIKES BACK!

BY TOMMY

It is a dark time at McQuarrie Middle School . . .

When did it start? I can tell you exactly when it started.

The first day of school. The very first day of seventh grade. We didn't even get one good day. We got, like, five minutes.

It was kind of like that scene where Han and Leia think they're going to breakfast with Lando. And they're walking down the hall thinking, "I'd like some chocolate chip pancakes," and then they get to the dining room and all of a sudden . . . there's Vader. (And no chocolate chip pancakes.)

So on the first morning of seventh grade, we were all hanging around the library—me and Sara, Kellen and Rhondella, Lance and Amy. It just felt like everything was perfect and the whole year was going to be perfect. We were all saying hello, and Kellen was introducing us to this sixth-grader he knew named Murky, and they were telling us this crazy story about what happened to them at the skate park over the summer because of Origami Yoda.

Then all of a sudden . . . there's Harvey.

"Paperwad Yoda? Sorry, this isn't the year of Paperwad Yoda."

And then he goes, "Bom bom bom bom-ba-bomb bom-ba-bomb." Vader's theme.

And he sticks out his hand and there it is: an origami Darth Vader, made out of black paper, with shiny silver eyes and a red paper lightsaber.

There are a lot of things that might have happened next. I was about to say, "That's awesome," because I did think it was awesome.

But before any of us guys could say anything like that, Rhondella says, "Aww, it's so cute!"

And Sara says, "Yeah, it really is cute, Harvey."

And Amy says, "He's so teeeny!"

Harvey was furious, of course. His voice got loud and high-pitched, which is always a bad sign with Harvey.

"Darth Paper is not cute!" he yelled.

"I love his little lightsaber!" Sara squealed.

"Will you make me a pink one?" asked Rhondella.

"I should have known you people would act like this!" hollered Harvey.

I tried to calm him down a bit. "Harvey, ree-lax. They're saying they like it. Here, let me get a good look at it."

I reached out for it, but he yanked it away.

"Shove it, Tommy," he snarled, and stomped off.

Then he turned around and held up Darth Paper and did a perfect Vader impression: "Do not underestimate the power of the Dark Side!"

Then he left.

"You guys are so weird," said Rhondella.

"What did WE do?" asked Kellen. "Don't blame us for—"

But Rhondella wasn't listening anymore, because some other girls had shown up and they were all hugging and saying "I missed you" and "Where did you go this summer?" and all that kind of stuff. Then they all sat down at one table, and we all sat down at the other table, and the perfect morning was over . . . and so was the perfect year.

You forgot to mention that I also do the Darth Vader breathing sound perfectly.

Tommy's Comment: Good grief! Not only did Harvey (and Vader) ruin everything, he even tricked me into letting him write his stupid comments again. Arrgh!

DARTH PAPER
✳ VS. ORIGAMI YODA

BY TOMMY

The good news is that Dwight showed up a little while later with Origami Yoda.

Last year, Origami Yoda did all kinds of stuff to make our lives better. Like, he got everyone to stop calling Quavondo "Cheeto Hog" and he got Mike to stop crying every time he struck out in P.E. And then there was the amazing miracle of making a school Fun Night actually fun. Origami Yoda helped me ask Sara to dance, and a bunch of us who have never danced before ended up doing this crazy move called the Twist.

The bad news is that this year Origami Yoda's up against the destructive force of Darth Paper, and can't seem to handle it.

It has all gone wrong since that first day. Now it's October and Darth Paper has pretty much destroyed all the good Origami Yoda did last year. Now the girls don't like us. The teachers don't like us. Some of us don't even like each other.

Sara, who I thought was practically my girlfriend, is going on a date with Tater Tot. That's right! Sara and Tater Tot!

Meanwhile, Rhondella won't talk to Kellen. Lance and Amy broke up. And Mike's crying in class again!

But it's been even worse for Dwight. He's been suspended from school, and the school board is going to decide if he should get sent to CREF—the Correctional and Remedial Education Facility—the school where they send the really, really bad kids, which Dwight isn't. Amy's older brother said the toughest, meanest, nastiest guy in his class was sent

WHERE'S MY ALIEN ROCK BAND?

there . . . and got beat up! It's kind of like Jabba's palace, except without the alien rock band.

This would be the ultimate defeat for Origami Yoda! And we think that Darth Paper is behind it. I just find it hard to believe that even Darth Paper/Harvey could be so evil!

So with Dwight out of school for almost two weeks now, the rest of us have gone back to being losers. Because, obviously, if Dwight's not here, Origami Yoda isn't here either, since Dwight is the one who goes around with Origami Yoda on his finger and makes him give advice.

Last year we tried to figure out if Origami Yoda was real. If he was using the Force or if Dwight was somehow playing a trick on us. But if you want to know more about that, you can read the first case file. This case file is for a different reason.

This case file is to try to save Dwight and Origami Yoda from the school board. How is

FIRST CASE FILE ← 30% LESS HARVEY!

it going to save them? I have no idea. But Origami Yoda said to do it, so we're doing it.

That was the last piece of advice Origami Yoda was able to give us. Since then we've been on our own. Actually, it's worse than that . . .

Instead of Dwight and Origami Yoda, we're stuck with Harvey and Darth Paper!

Harvey's Comment

Stuck with Darth Paper? Fools! If you had only joined Darth Paper . . . we could have ruled this entire school! Paperwad Yoda's pitiful advice is nothing compared to the power of the Dark Side!

My Comment: See what I mean?

NOTE: THIS IS NOT JABBA'S ALIEN ROCK BAND. IT'S ACTUALLY THE 8TH-GRADE CHORUS!!!

TOMMY

HOW WE GOT INTO THIS MESS

BY TOMMY

So Darth Paper and Origami Yoda were always fighting.

At first, Harvey wanted them to have an actual fight with paper lightsabers, but Dwight wouldn't do it.

"Wars do not make one great," Dwight/Origami Yoda said.

But he ended up fighting a war whether he wanted to or not. Harvey wouldn't let up.

He and Darth Paper would do something obnoxious—like find out I was doing a report

PAPER LIGHTSABER

CUT LONG TRIANGLE

FOLD BOTTOM

PRESTO!
(WATCH OUT FOR PAPER CUTS!)

GOOD BOOK →

on Booker T. Washington and run to the library and check out all the books about him. But then Origami Yoda would come up with a solution— like telling me that you can download Booker T. Washington's autobiography for free.

Origami Yoda and Darth Paper spent the whole first month battling each other like that.

Then all of a sudden things got bad so fast, we could barely even figure out what was going on.

It started when Jen came over to our lunch table to ask Origami Yoda a question.

Jen is one of the people who never talked to us before Origami Yoda. And because she's so popular, we figured she must be a real stuck-up. But actually, once we got to know her a little better, she didn't seem so bad. And she took Origami Yoda pretty seriously, which was really surprising. It turns out that she is a huge *Star Wars* fan.

"Need some help from Darth Paper?" asked Harvey.

JEN →

"Uh, no," she answered. "I need some real Jedi Master advice. See, they're going to let me try out for the JV cheerleading team at the high school. It's usually just eighth- and ninth-graders. It's super-hard for a seventh-grader to make it. I'm totally practicing all the time. Do you think Origami Yoda can give me any secret advice?"

Dwight was just sort of staring at his food. He's been kind of depressed since Caroline, this girl he really liked, started going to this private school, Tippett Academy. So Dwight was moping around a lot, but he was still willing to let us ask Origami Yoda questions, which proves he's a really nice guy. He raised a finger, and there was Origami Yoda, ready to go.

Now, since Jen had said she was going to TRY out, Kellen and I both expected Origami Yoda to say, "No, try not. Do or do not. There is no try," which is a famous Yoda line from the best movie ever, *The Empire Strikes Back.*

R REAL YODA!

Instead, Dwight got this really, really weird look on his face. He stood up and moved toward Jen. He put Origami Yoda right in her face.

This was strange, even for Dwight.

Then he got even stranger. He spoke in Yoda's voice. He usually does a terrible Yoda impression, but this time he sounded just like Yoda after Luke comes out of the dream cave and Yoda gets all scary.

"Zero Hour comes . . . ," he muttered.

"What—," Jen started to say.

"Zero Hour comes. Prepare to meet your Doom!"

"Dude, you don't have to be all weird about it," Jen said, and took off. The look on her face made me figure that was the last time she was ever going to ask Origami Yoda a question.

"Man, that was totally disturbed," said Harvey.

For once I couldn't argue with him. The

whole thing had seemed extremely Dark Side of the Force.

"I think you'd better go apologize to her," I said to Dwight. "That was way too scary. She might think you meant it like a threat or something."

"Yeah, Dwight, you could get in trouble for something like that," said Kellen.

So far Dwight hadn't said anything or even sat back down. But as soon as Kellen said the word "trouble," Dwight sat down, put Origami Yoda in his pocket, and started pushing his thumb into his hamburger over and over really hard.

"Why do you say stuff like that, man?" Kellen asked.

"I didn't say it," Dwight mumbled. "Origami Yoda did."

"Well, I'm going to give her another chance to listen to Darth Paper," said Harvey, and he went off after Jen.

We thought that was going to be the end

of it. Yes, Dwight was weirder than usual, but it didn't seem like THAT big of a deal. I mean, we didn't think he was going to get kicked out of school because of it. So we all just finished our lunch, the bell rang, and we went to class.

We don't know exactly what happened next, because no one will tell us anything. Principal Rabbski says it isn't our business, but I think it is.

RABBSKI!

Anyway, somewhere in there Jen must have told somebody—maybe Principal Rabbski—that Dwight had said something scary. Maybe she even said that it sounded like a threat.

Kellen was in class with Dwight when Dwight got called to the office. Dwight has gotten sent to the office about a bajillion times, so it wasn't that big of a deal for him to get called out of class.

But then he didn't come back. We heard he was in in-school suspension all day. Then in eighth period, Sara told us she had seen

Dwight's mom in the hall heading toward the office.

So when school was over, Kellen and I went down there to see if we could figure out what was going on.

We got there just in time.

We had, like, five seconds to talk to Dwight when he came out of the office. His mother was still inside talking to Principal Rabbski.

Dwight looked like a zombie. He was too freaked out to say anything.

But he held up Yoda, and Yoda said, "Out of school kicked we have been."

"Kicked out? For what? For having Yoda? No way!" said Kellen.

"Way yes," croaked Yoda. "Save Dwight you must."

"How?"

"The truth for the school board you must write. Another case file is needed."

I was going to ask him something useful about <u>the</u> case file—like, why we needed to write it or what it should be about—when Kellen butted in.

"Should I doodle on it again?" asked Kellen annoyingly.

"Hurt that could not, I guess," answered Yoda.

Then Dwight's mother and Principal Rabbski came out of the office, and I didn't have a chance to ask my useful question.

Dwight's mother was all worked up. Crying and sniffling.

"Oh, Dwight, please! Put your origami away," she pleaded. "We've got to go."

Principal Rabbski glared at us. "Tommy and Kellen, I really don't think Dwight needs any more encouragement from you two right now."

As Dwight and his mother left, Rabbski started a little lecture about how we had "contributed" to Dwight's problems. Kellen and I tried to ask her what was going on, but she said that disciplinary matters are private and she wouldn't talk to us.

As soon as I got home from school, I e-mailed Dwight. Here's his reply:

What are they having for lunch tomorrow? Origami Yoda thinks a Rib-B-Q sandwich it is. If so, will you buy one for me and get Sara to bring it home with her and then give it to me?

RIB
-B-
Q →

That told me absolutely nothing (although it turned out he was right about the Rib-B-Q)! However, the e-mail had an attachment, and it was a jpeg of a scanned-in letter from Principal Rabbski!

ZAck

I couldn't believe it. A "history of violent behavior"? Yes, Dwight got suspended last year after his fight with Zack. But since when is standing up to a bully a "history of violent behavior"? Zack's the one who should get sent to CREF, I thought. Dwight would never hurt anybody. He says stuff like "Zero Hour comes" all the time. It's not a threat, it's just Dwight.

LUCAS COUNTY BOARD OF EDUCATION
REQUEST FOR CREF REFERRAL

SCHOOL: McQuarrie Middle
PRINCIPAL: L. Rabbski

STUDENT: Dwight Tharp
STUDENT ID#: 69735-D-43
GRADE: 7

REASON: Students have come to me with concerns about threatening speech/bullying. In addition to violating our zero-tolerance policy on bullying, this is an especial concern because of Dwight's history of violent behavior—behavior for which he was suspended last year.

Additionally, Dwight has shown a pattern of disrespect for authority and is a continual disruption to the learning environment. We have used every disciplinary tool available to us to stop his many unacceptable behaviors—which include frequent use of a finger puppet—but have not succeeded. We believe Dwight would best be served by the special attention available at CREF.

Recommendation: I have no choice but to ask the Board to place Dwight Tharp at CREF for at least the remainder of the semester.

To be presented at the Oct. 28 Board of Education meeting.

I realized then that the new case file Origami Yoda asked for must be for us to show the school board at that meeting on October 28. If they just listen to Rabbski, they'll think Dwight is some kind of nut.

Well, I mean, he is a nut, I guess. But he's a good kind of nut. And that's what we have to tell the school board.

So I've decided that we need to collect stories that show that Dwight and Origami Yoda are good and good to have at school. (Come on, people—Yoda would never be a bad guy! That's just dumb.) We have to prove that Dwight doesn't belong with the bad kids.

By the way, when I say "we," I mean me and Kellen (and various other people too), but I do not mean Harvey.

NO HARVEY!

Did you notice that Mrs. Rabbski said that "students" came to her with concerns? So it wasn't just Jen; it was Jen plus somebody else. I don't have any proof, but I bet I know who . . . Harvey. That's one of the things

I'm hoping to figure out. Part of the "truth"
Origami Yoda wants us to find.

Harvey's Comment

Don't blame me! I tried and tried to get Dwight to
throw that Paperwad Yoda away, and he wouldn't
do it. And who was it that got Dwight in trouble?
Paperwad Yoda, that's who.

My Comment: Yeah, right.

Anyway, here are the stories we've collected
to defend Dwight. Some show that he's a nice
guy. Some show that Harvey's a jerk. Hopefully,
when we put them all together, they'll show
the school board that Dwight and Origami Yoda
are not dangerous or a disruption or anything
like that. I sure hope they work . . .

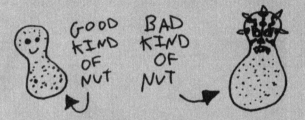

IN DEFENSE OF DWIGHT AND ORIGAMI YODA

BY TOMMY AND KELLEN

Dear School Board Members,

You have GOT to let Dwight come back to school.

For one thing, he is our friend, and we miss having him around—even if he does embarrass us sometimes.

For another thing, we need him. He's a good guy and helps us with our problems.

Now, you may think it's strange that he helps us by letting us talk to the Yoda finger puppet he made. So what? He still helps us.

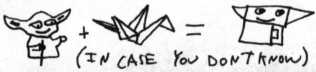

(IN CASE YOU DON'T KNOW)

Back in the sixth grade, he did all kinds of stuff for us—mostly keeping us from making fools of ourselves. But he also got Sara and Rhondella to dance with us at a Fun Night.

So we thought we were going to start a new year with girlfriends—or almost girlfriends—and with perfect advice for any problem we had. It was going to be awesome.

We know it may sound weird to you all, but we had gotten to the point where we had started to think that talking to a finger puppet was pretty normal.

So what you are wondering is: If Dwight is such a good guy, why is he in trouble?

Well, we blame this kid named Harvey. You'll be hearing a lot about him. If you decided to send HIM to CREF, it would be fine with us.

He has always hated Origami Yoda, especially after Yoda made a fool of him at that Fun Night last year. So this year he made an origami Darth Vader to fight with Yoda.

Now, we do have to admit that sometimes Dwight gets into trouble all by himself.

23

But not for doing bad stuff—just weird stuff. Like that time he brought that giant yo-yo to English class for an oral report and busted a light with it and lightbulb pieces went everywhere and the teacher evacuated the room because she thought that lightbulbs were filled with toxic gas.

That's why we're always telling him to ask Origami Yoda before he does stuff. Origami Yoda would have said, "Do that giant yo-yo trick directly under a light you must not." Or something like that.

Anyway, that wasn't Dwight being bad—just Dwight making a weird mistake.

And even though what got Dwight into trouble sounds bad, we think it was just a weird mistake too. I'm sure Principal Rabbski has told you all about what Origami Yoda said to Jen. We can't explain to you why he said that stuff about "Zero Hour" and "Doom," but we can tell you that we don't think he meant anything bad. And neither do the other kids at school.

So we all got together to make this case file that has a bunch of stories that show that Dwight and Origami Yoda have not gone over to the Dark Side! They are the good guys!

Sincerely,

Tommy Lomax

KELLEN CAMPBELL

SARA BOLT

RHondella CarRasQuillo

lance alexander

Mike coLey

Jacob cornelius

Quavondo Phan

Amy youmans

Cassie Dillon

murky Kahleel

Remi Minnick

Ben Man TRue

Caroline Broome

James Suero

KELLEN

ORIGAMI YODA AND THE BRAT

BY KELLEN
(AS DICTATED TO TOMMY)

Dear School Board Members,

This shows the way that Dwight and Origami Yoda help us solve problems, even though it actually happened over the summer, not at school. In this case, Origami Yoda saved the life of a small child!

Because otherwise I was going to strangle the little brat!

I'm just kidding, of course! I wasn't really going to kill him or even hurt him. That was the problem. He was too small to beat up.

But

Everybody would have said I was a monster for picking on a little kid.

He may be little, but he's got a big, nasty mouth.

All this happened at the Vinton skate park this summer. My mom would drop me off there on her way to work and pick me up on her way home. I had spent months begging and pleading for this arrangement and had done a million random chores to show that I was "responsible and mature enough."

It should have been paradise. Hanging out with my friends, practicing tricks, getting junk food and Mountain Dews at the Qwikpick right across Route 24.

The whole problem was that the Brat lived nearby and just walked over. You never knew when he was going to show up. And once he was there, he would never, ever leave!

Here's how my summer started:

I was dying to show Lance and Murky my 50-50 grind. I'd been working on it every chance I could get.

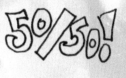

I drop into the bowl, get great compression, and come up for the grind. But instead of the board grinding the lip, it slipped sideways too fast. My feet came off, and I fell back into the bowl, cracked my shin just under the knee pad, scraped the heck out of my left hand, and clonked my helmet pretty hard.

I'm lying there for a second, wondering if I'm dead, when this loud, high-pitched, obnoxious voice comes screeching across the bowl: "Dude, you suck."

I look up and see this tiny figure silhouetted against the angry summer sun. It was the Brat!

Lance and Murky—who should have been jumping into the bowl to see if I was OK—started giggling.

What was the rest of the summer like? Basically like that, over and over again. Try to practice something hard, and if you don't land it every time, it's "You suck!" or "Fail!" If you do nail a trick, the Brat is like, "That wasn't so high" or "Tony Hawk does it better."

You can't get away from him. As you know, it's the only skate park in town, and it's pretty small. There's the bowl, a couple rails, and a mini quarter pipe for beginners. That's it. Whatever you do, he's always right there to see it and complain about it.

And here's the worst part. The Brat couldn't actually skate. He just walked around with a helmet and pads and a board, which didn't have a scratch on them!

It doesn't do any good to tell him off, either. He goes, "Don't get mad at me just because you bailed!"

Everybody hated him, but I think I hated him most because he seemed to rag on me more than on anybody else.

So, anyway, after a couple weeks, I was ready to whack him in the head with my board.

"You can't do that, stooky," said Murky while we were getting Mountain Dews at the

Bowl

RAILS

MINI

PLACE
WHERE
SUB
BOX
WAS
B-4
IT
FELL
APART

29

Qwikpick with Lance. ("Stooky" is a Murky-ism. It means kind of like "dude.") "He's obnoxious, but he's just a little kid."

"Plus, I think he can probably beat you up, man," Lance added.

MURKY

LANCE

"Very funny, Lance," I said. "Obviously, I'm not going to hit the little brat, but I've got to do something. I'm actually thinking of going to day camp with my sisters," I said.

"Day camp? Are you serious?" asked Lance.

"You'd go crazy there," said Murky.

"Well, I'm already going crazy here. I can't take that brat anymore. What am I going to do?"

"Ask Origami Yoda," said a voice. And a hand appeared over the chips rack and it had Origami Yoda on one finger.

Suddenly, I had a New Hope!

"Is that you, Dwight?"

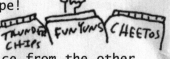

"Yes," came Dwight's voice from the other side. "I was browsing the pork-rind selection—which, by the way, is exceptional here—when I overheard your problem. I think Origami Yoda can help."

"What the heck?" Murky was half saying, half laughing.

But Lance and I were like, "Shhh, dude, Origami Yoda is totally Jedi wise."

"Origami Yoda, what can I do about the Brat?" I asked. I told him what had been going on.

The little green finger puppet started wiggling. And we heard a creaky, squeaky voice. "Teach him you must."

"That's what I wanted to do. Teach him upside his head with my board."

"No!" goes Yoda. "To skateboard, teach him you must."

"What? No way!"

"Way yes," said Yoda.

I went around to the next aisle to tell Dwight what a stupid idea this was. But Dwight wasn't there! Neither was Yoda. Just the pork rinds.

"What did he do, teleport?" said Murky.

"Actually, he's probably in the bathroom," said Lance.

The men's room door was closed. Lance checked it. It was locked.

"Are you in there, Dwight?" I yelled.

No answer. We waited a few minutes to see if he would come out, but he didn't. So we paid for our stuff and left.

When we got back to the park, the Brat was being a brat like usual.

"You got to do it," said Lance. "Origami Yoda is always right."

"Yeah, I know, but if I teach him to skate, he'll just keep coming!"

"Maybe he'll fall on his butt and run home crying and never come back," said Murky. "Problem solved."

Well, I did teach him, and he did fall on his butt and cry. But he didn't run home.

We kept working on it. Every morning before

the place got crowded, I'd help him do drop-
ins off the mini quarter pipe. Once he learned
that, I taught him to ride up the ramp and
come back down. Then how to do a Rock 'n' Roll
on the lip.

You might think I'm going to tell you that
he learned fast and got really good, but he
didn't. The truth is, he sucks. But I never
tell him that. And he never tells me I suck
anymore, either.

Harvey's Comment

How come there's always a story about Dwight in the bathroom?

My Comment: Great . . . Harvey just has to have the
case file so he can add his "scientific" comments to it,
and this is what we get: bathroom jokes.

That reminds me . . . The Brat reminds me of
someone. Let's see . . . a kid who just stands around and
complains and insults people all the time? I just can't

think who that reminds me of . . . (cough) Harvey (cough).

In fact, the next story is all about the complaining and the insults, with the extra-annoying bonus of Darth Paper!

ORIGAMI YODA AND THE HUMMINGBIRD HAWK MOTH

BY SARA

Dear School Board,

It's weird that I'm the one who's going to tell you this story, but in a weird way I'm the one who caused it. Sort of a butterfly effect. That thing about how a butterfly flapping its wings somewhere can cause a snowstorm somewhere else? You know what I'm talking about? Actually, I guess you'd call it the "moth effect" for this story.

What happened was that on the first day of school Mrs. Porterfield, our biology teacher, let us choose which table we'd sit at. Each table has two seats, and whoever you sit with is going to be your partner on stuff.

So, when I walk in the room, most of the chairs are taken, but nobody is sitting with Dwight. It's no surprise that no one was sitting with him. I don't say that to be mean, because he IS a friend of mine. I've gotten to know him by living next door to him. But most normal people don't know him and don't really want to know him.

AMY

So I was willing to sit with him and I was moving in his direction, but then Amy popped up from a desk at the front of the room and called my name. She had saved a seat for me.

I could have kept going and sat with Dwight and this story never would have happened. But that would have been really rude to Amy, so I turned and went back to sit with her, which was just a tiny bit rude to Dwight, but he didn't even seem to notice.

So when the last person came to class, the seat next to Dwight was the only seat left. And guess who the last person was? Harvey.

Now, most people would have just accepted it and sat down next to Dwight. They would have complained about it later, but they wouldn't have said anything in front of Dwight.

Not Harvey.

"You've got to be kidding me!" he says really loud. "Is that seriously the only seat left?"

Frankly, I think most people were glad it was the last seat, because for them sitting with Harvey would be even worse than sitting with Dwight.

"Harvey, please take your seat," said Mrs. Porter-field.

"This isn't a permanent seating arrangement, is it?" he whined. "I'm not going to be stuck here all year, am I?"

MRS. PORTERFIELD

"I'm sure I could find a seat for you in Principal Rabbski's office," said Mrs. Porterfield.

She turned out to be pretty good at making jokes like this.

Harvey made this big, ridiculous sigh and flopped down next to Dwight.

"Just don't bug me," he said to Dwight.

"Actually," said Mrs. Porterfield, "we're all going to be bugging each other a lot for the next few weeks. Can anybody guess why?"

Nobody could guess.

"Because our first unit is going to be insects. And we're going to be going outside a lot to collect insects while the weather is still nice."

"Nice?" whined Harvey. "It's ninety-five degrees out there."

"Once again, Harvey," Mrs. Porterfield said, "I'd like to point out that if you find the principal's office more comfortable, I can arrange for you to spend a lot of time there."

I was starting to like Mrs. Porterfield. Maybe she would be the person who was finally able to get Harvey to shut up.

The next day we started our bug "collections."

Mrs. Porterfield said that when she was learning biology, people had jars of poison that they used to kill the bugs they caught. Then they used pins to stick them in boxes.

Apparently, the school system had decided that the poison wasn't safe and neither were the pins. Plus Mrs. Porterfield said it is a lot easier to appreciate nature when it is still alive.

So she had a digital camera with this weird attachment on it. When you caught a bug, you put it in this little plastic bubble, and the camera took a close-up photo of it. Then you could let the bug go and put the bug's picture on a Flickr page she set up for our class.

"If you each catch at least three bugs, we'll have seventy-five pictures. But the hard part is catching seventy-five DIFFERENT bugs. We don't want seventy-five pictures of the same kind of ant."

All of a sudden, Dwight sticks his hand up—not to ask a question. He's got Origami Yoda on his finger, and Origami Yoda says, "A hummingbird hawk moth, catch it we will."

I've noticed that when Dwight uses Origami Yoda, he talks a little bit different depending on whether Yoda is giving an order, stating a fact, or predicting the future. This was definitely the more spacey prediction voice.

Harvey goes, "Ha."

Then he holds up Darth Paper: "Your powers are weak. You'll never catch a hummingbird hawk moth."

"Well," said Mrs. Porterfield, as if it was completely normal to have talking finger puppets in her class. "It is true that hummingbird hawk moths are somewhat uncommon. However, a student last year did catch a regular hawk moth."

"A hummingbird hawk moth, find it we will," said Origami Yoda, using the stating-a-fact voice.

"Look, Dwight," said Harvey, in his normal whiny voice. "I went to nature camp this summer and studied entomology for two weeks, and nobody in the class even SAW a hummingbird hawk moth the whole time."

"A hummingbird hawk moth, see it we will," said Origami Yoda, now in the command voice.

Darth Paper goes, "Your brain is weak too, old man!"

"All right, already," said Mrs. Porterfield. "Let's not waste any more time talking about which bugs we'll find. Let's go outside and start looking. There's no use worrying about any particular bug, Dwight. Whatever bug you catch will be useful, not just a hummingbird hawk moth."

Each team got a net, and we all went out back to look for bugs around the edges of the soccer field. It was pretty hot out there, but it was fun.

"If you catch a bee, just keep it in your net until I

can help you with it!" called Mrs. Porterfield as we all started running around. Everybody except Dwight and Harvey, that is. They were still standing by the doors arguing over who would get to use the net.

Amy and I were the first team to catch a bug. It was a butterfly. Mrs. Porterfield took a picture of it and said we'd use a field guide to identify it later.

"It's an orange skipper," said Harvey.

"OK, Harvey," said Mrs. Porterfield. "You need to catch your own bug instead of interrupting the other teams."

"How can I catch my own bug when Dwight won't let me have the net?"

Mrs. Porterfield sighed, and I was so glad that I wasn't stuck with Harvey.

It went on like this for the whole week. Everybody catching bugs and Harvey complaining and trying to identify other people's bugs and saying, "You'll never catch a hummingbird hawk moth" to Dwight over and over and over.

Dwight turned out to be the best bug catcher. I noticed

that instead of running around he moved really, really slowly and then suddenly—*swoosh!*—he'd catch one.

But even though Dwight caught seven different kinds of butterflies and a praying mantis, he didn't catch a hummingbird hawk moth.

When Dwight caught something, Harvey would paw at the net and then shout: "A yellow swallowtail. I told you it wouldn't be a hummingbird hawk moth!"

We all got sick of hearing it. I mean, Harvey seemed to think that the only thing any of us cared about was whether Dwight caught a hummingbird hawk moth or not.

By the end of the week we DID care. Amy and me and some of the others were all trying to catch one too, so that we could secretly give it to Dwight.

But by Friday no one had even seen one. In fact, I really wasn't sure what they looked like.

Then, with like ten minutes to go, we're all running around trying to catch one and Dwight is just standing still, holding his net. Harvey had given up on taking turns with Dwight and was trying to catch bugs with his bare hands by flipping over rocks.

All of a sudden there's this *buzzzzzzzzzzzzzz* and a *WHIP* with the net, and Dwight's got something. He calmly walks over to Mrs. Porterfield.

Now, some kids didn't care, but Amy and me and a couple others were dying to find out if it was a hummingbird hawk moth. Whatever it was, it was huge and still buzzing. Mrs. Porterfield was having some trouble getting it out of the net into the camera thing. Then she does, and it sits in the bubble completely still, and it's amazingly beautiful, with shiny clear wings and this weird long coiled-up nose and a big fat, fuzzy body.

"What is it?" asks Harvey, trying to look over my shoulder.

"It's a hummingbird hawk moth, Darth Smarty-Pants," says Mrs. Porterfield.

The next day, Mrs. Porterfield hung up a printout of the picture of the hummingbird hawk moth, and it's still hanging up there. And Harvey has finally shut up—at least in biology class.

That is totally not the way it really happened. But you're not interested in the truth anymore. Here's the truth: Anybody who got stuck with Dwight as a lab partner would end up complaining.

My Comment: Dwight seems like a good partner to me. He caught a lot of bugs. And you both ended up getting an A on the bug collection.

I just wish it had been me sitting with Sara. I barely get to see her this year!

MIKE

ORIGAMI YODA AND THE NON-VIDEO GAME

BY MIKE

Dear School Board,

Every morning me and my friends Lance, Hannah, and Murky spend the time before school on the computers in the library playing this awesome online game: Clone Wars StrikeTeam. We all play at the same time and have to cooperate to win.

Other kids, like Harvey, Remi, and Ben play stuff too, or check e-mails or whatever. It's a fun way to start the school day.

Or at least, it was!

Oh, and we also learned valuable lessons about teamwork, planning, math, hand-eye coordination,

LET'S COOPERATE!

LET'S LEARN VALUABLE LESSONS!

and other important skills that aided in our education and probably improved our performance on the Standards of Learning tests.

Then one day about a month ago, we go into the library and there are signs all over that say:

NO E-MAIL

NO CHAT

NO FACEBOOK

NO VIDEO GAMES!!!

We sat down to play anyway but couldn't get on to the website. That's when Mrs. Calhoun came over and told us that the new library policy was no games. She said the Clone Wars site had been blocked, and so had some others. She also said that if we found a game site that wasn't blocked, we couldn't play that either, and if she caught us, she'd throw us out of the library.

MRS. CALHOUN

I started to argue with her, which was a bad idea because sometimes I get worked up when I get in an argument.

Mrs. Calhoun sent me to the office to see Principal Rabbski. Rabbski said she was disappointed to see

I'M JUST A BIT WORKED UP!

me crying over video games and that maybe some in-school suspension time would help me calm down. I tried to explain the difference between mad tears and boo-hoo tears. Nobody ever listens!

Rabbski told me this wasn't the librarian's decision anyway—it was you school board members who had made that policy.

So, first of all, we would like you to change the no-games policy. The games we play are very strategic and educational. Kind of like chess, just with lightsabers and stuff.

Second, I'll tell you what happened next.

While I was in ISS, I realized that I should have gotten Origami Yoda's advice before I did anything.

I got out of ISS in time for lunch, and me and Murky went over to see Dwight.

"Origami Yoda, how can we get Mrs. Calhoun to let us play games again?"

"Let you play games she will."

"No, she won't! She put up a sign."

"Saw that sign I did. No VIDEO games it said."

"Yeah, that's what I said."

WE'RE BACK!

BOO-HOO

MAD

"Other kinds of games there are."

"What, you mean playing chess or something? That's boring."

"Chess is not boring," said Dwight.

"Well, compared with Clone Wars StrikeTeam, it is. And don't forget they already banned card games. No Magic, no Pokémon."

"There is another," Yoda said really mystically, "type of game. Mr. Snider you must ask."

Mr. Snider was my English teacher last year. He was a nice guy, so I figured it couldn't hurt to ask him.

We went by his room after school. He told us that when he was a kid back in the 1970s, you couldn't play video games at school because they didn't have computers. And they hadn't invented Pokémon back then, either.

But they did have Star Wars, he told us, and he and his friends played this Star Wars game.

MR. SNIDER

"Man, I haven't thought about that game in years," he said.

He got out some paper and drew the Death Star

48

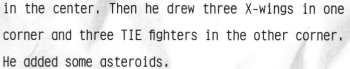

in the center. Then he drew three X-wings in one corner and three TIE fighters in the other corner. He added some asteroids.

"Uh, this is a game?" said Murky.

"Yeah—hold on," said Mr. Snider, and he pulled a pencil out of a drawer.

"You want to be Rebels or Empire?"

"Rebels," said Murky.

"OK, I'll take the TIE fighters then," said Mr. Snider. He put the pencil tip on top of a TIE fighter, then rested his finger on the eraser so the pencil stood straight up. Then he squinted at the paper. He moved his other hand into position and flicked his index finger real quick against the pencil, down near the bottom.

The pencil went flying and left behind a mark on the paper about an inch long.

"Hmm, I've lost my touch," he said. "But you see how it works? If you hit another ship with your 'shot,' you've blown that ship up. If not, you move your ship to the end of the mark. First person to blow up all the other guy's ships wins."

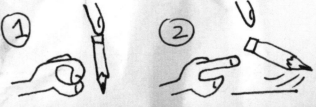

There were some more rules: Hit the Death Star and your ship is blown up. Hit an asteroid and your ship loses a turn.

He picked up the pencil and gave it to Murky. "Your turn," he said.

I watched as they had a space fight all around the Death Star. I couldn't wait for them to finish, so Hannah and I started our own game. It was pretty awesome.

See, you can't just go firing away like you do in a video game. Because if you miss the other guy by an inch, then your ship gets moved so that it's an inch away from the other guy—and he blasts you easy the next time. It really does take strategy.

So that was the beginning of the Pencil Wars. A bunch of other people have started playing too, and we've added all kinds of extra rules and special ships and players you can use and stuff.

Plus Mr. S told us about another pencil game that they called Obstacle Course, and Murky realized it was perfect for Podracing. Man, it's so cool to

have a game with four people all trying to flick their Podracers through Beggar's Canyon without hitting the walls or each other!

I mean, I still want you school board people to let us play on the computers again, but until then, this is an awesome solution.

Harvey's Comment

Yeah, and it's "awesome" to try to study in the library while a bunch of idiots are flicking pencils and shouting, "Ooh, ooh, I got you."

The pencil games stink! Bring back the computer games!

My Comment: Harvey's just mad because the one time he played, Hannah blew up all his TIE fighters before he could even get one of her X-wings.

I don't want to get back into the whole "Is Origami Yoda real" thing, but it sure is weird that Mr. Snider told them he hadn't thought about playing that game in years. So how could Yoda/Dwight have known about it?

Anyway, I think the school board will like this one because it shows Dwight helping people to find something better to do than either play video games or complain about not playing video games. Our guidance counselor is always talking about "positive solutions." Well, this is one. The next one is too. I just wish I'd gotten in on it.

STEP 1 - MAKE A GAME BOARD

STEP 2 - TAKE TURNS SHOOTING + MOVING YOUR SHIPS... IF YOU HIT AN ENEMY SHIP IT BLOWS UP!

STEP 3 OTHERWISE... MOVE YOUR SHIP TO THE END OF THE PENCIL MARK...

WATCH OUT FOR ASTEROIDS + BAD GUYS

STEP 4 BLOW UP ALL THE OTHER GUY'S SHIPS TO WIN!

VARIATIONS....

FALCON'S SHIELDS CAN SURVIVE 1 HIT

VADER'S TIE CAN FIRE/MOVE TWICE PER TURN!

LANCE

ORIGAMI YODA AND EXPLODING PIZZA BAGELS OF LOVE

BY LANCE

Dear School Board,

This story is really weird, because Origami Yoda gave me the advice last year—but I didn't understand why it was so good until this year.

See, just before the end of sixth grade we got to choose which seventh-grade elective course we would take this year.

I couldn't decide between model rocketry and LEGO robots. On the one hand, I already have a LEGO robot set at home and have done some cool stuff with it, so I thought that class would be fun. On the other hand,

SIZZLER!

I've always wanted to shoot off a model rocket, but my mother said no way. But I asked her if she would please let me take the class, since Mrs. Budzinski would make sure I didn't blow myself up. She said OK!

But I still couldn't make up my mind, so I decided to ask Dwight and Origami Yoda. I stopped by the nerd table at lunch. I'm a nerd too, I guess, but I can't stand sitting at their table because one of them gets on my nerves real bad.

"Hey, guys and Origami Yoda," I said. "Which do you think I should sign up for—LEGO robots or model rocketry?"

Dwight said I might not be able to get into model rocketry, because everybody tries to sign up for model rocketry.

Then a second later he answered himself, but in his really bad Yoda-imitation voice.

"Alphabetically they will choose," said Origami Yoda. "Lance Alexander, pick anything he may."

"You mean that just because my last name starts with A, I can choose any class? Awesome," I said. "So which should I pick: rockets or LEGOs?"

"Family and consumer sciences pick should you, erm?" said Yoda.

"What's that?"

"That's like cooking and sewing and how to use coupons," said Kellen.

"Oh, you mean home ec. Isn't that just for girls?" I asked.

"Excuse me?" yelled Rhondella from the next table. "NO, it's not just for girls. It's for anybody who doesn't want to be a clueless idiot when they finish school."

And the way she and the other girls glared at me, you could tell they would vote for me as Most Likely to Be a Clueless Idiot. I don't mind Rhondella glaring at me, but it was awful to see Amy glaring at me. I kind of thought Amy liked me.

So by now I was pretty confused. The next day in homeroom, when Mr. Howell handed out the forms for us to pick our elective, I just couldn't decide.

I turned around to ask Dwight if he was sure about home ec. He was already folding his form into Admiral Ackbar.

"Dwight," I whispered. "Why home ec?"

He held up Origami Yoda and began, "Erm…"

"Dwight!" shouted Mr. Howell. "How many times do

MR. HOWELL →

I have to tell you to put that puppet away? And what are you doing to your form?"

"Commence attack on the Death Star's main reactor," said Origami Admiral Ackbar.

Howell yelled for a little while, then sent Dwight to in-school suspension.

"The rest of you, pass your forms up to the front," he snarled at us.

I had no more time and no more help from Yoda.

But I'm a believer. I put a checkmark next to "family and consumer sciences."

So that was last year. What happened? Did I actually like family and consumer sciences better than I would have liked LEGO robots or model rockets?

Well, hold on—I'll tell you. When I got to class on the first day, there were just two guys in it. Me and Tater Tot. Well, we're not great friends or anything, but I figured we would sit at a table together and be cooking partners or whatever. Forget it. He never even glanced at me; he sat down next to Sara!

Then Amy came in and she saw that the seat next to Sara was taken. And then she looked at me. And we

OH, LANCE! LET ME MAKE BAGELS WITH YOU, HOTSTUFF!

sat down together and have done every project together since then. And she's never looked at me like I
was a Clueless Idiot again, except for the time our pizza
bagels blew up in the microwave because I put them
in for 3:00 instead of 0:30. But then she laughed and
helped me clean it up.

Harvey's Comment

Thank Boba Fett I didn't take that class!!! If I had
to watch Lance and Amy making goo-goo eyes while
scraping pizza sauce out of the microwave, I'd barf
my brains out.

Do you want to know the truth behind this
mysterious prediction of Paperwad Yoda?

Dwight was afraid he wouldn't get into model
rocketry, since his last name is Tharp. So he
talked Lance out of it and probably some other
idiots too, and guess what? Dwight got into model
rocketry.

My Comment: Hmm, that's true about Dwight getting
into model rocketry. But frankly, I wish Origami Yoda

had told ME to take home ec so that I could be sitting with Sara instead of that jerky Tater Tot!

How am I supposed to get her to be my girlfriend when I hardly get to see her and Tater Tot gets to sit around making pizza bagels with her every day?

I USED TO THINK HOWELL LOOKED LIKE JABBA... BUT NOW I REALIZE HE LOOKS MORE LIKE A RANCOR!

MURKY!

ORIGAMI YODA AND YODA

BY MAHIR KAHLEEL (AKA MURKY)

School Board,

The other day after I watched *Empire Strikes Back* for the millionth time—massively bolt movie!!!!!!—I was thinking about Yoda. See, if he was 900 years old in *Empire Strikes Back*, then he was, like, 870 years old in *Phantom Menace*. So what was he doing all that time before the movies, and where did he come from??????

So I looked it up on Wookieepedia . . . and there's some stuff, but apparently nobody really knows!!!!! George Lucas won't say, and he won't let any other *Star Wars* writers come up with an answer either. But then I thought maybe I didn't need George Lucas after all. I go to school with Origami Yoda. If anybody knows, he would!!!

So I asked him.

ME: Where are you from? And I don't mean Dagobah. I
mean, where are you originally from?

ORIGAMI YODA: A tree.

ME: What? You mean, your species lives in trees? Like
monkeys? Or Ewoks?

ORIGAMI YODA: No. From a tree I come. Then from Asami
Origami Paper Company.

ME: Oh.

ANNOYING 7TH-GRADER NAMED HARVEY: Aha! The truth!
The truth at last! Origami Yoda himself admits he's
just a piece of paper.

KELLEN'S FRIEND TOMMY: Yeah, but for the first time,
you've acknowledged his existence. You just said,
"Origami Yoda himself admits."

HARVEY: Ha. Ha. You know what I mean. Whoever said it,
he's still just a piece of wood pulp from a sawed-up
tree. No magic Force, just tree.

ORIGAMI YODA: The Force flows through all living things
it does . . . plants and animals . . . people and
Wookiees and trees.

HARVEY: Whatever.

ME: What about the real Yoda?

HARVEY: There is no real Yoda, he's just a—

ME: Dude, would you shut up for a minute?

HARVEY: Why should I shut up? This is my table. If you don't like to listen to me, then don't stand around my table.

KELLEN: It's not YOUR table, Harvey, it's—

HARVEY [puts a Darth Vader puppet on his finger]: Don't make me destroy you!

ORIGAMI YODA: Noisy it is here. Come, let us to the freezer line go.

We went and got in the line to get Popsicles.

ORIGAMI YODA: Keep a secret can you? Never tell?

ME: Sure. Absolutely.

And Origami Yoda whispered the answer in my ear, and it was the total stooky stuff!!! Really fits with the whole rest of the Star Wars story and makes sense but is surprising, too.

And I've kept my promise to keep it a secret.

Give me a break! Am I supposed to believe that? Is there any point to this at all other than to prove that Murky should have been held back a year? or two? "Massively bolt"? "Total stooky stuff"? Does that even mean anything?

My Comment: That means it was really amazing, I think. But yeah, I'm not sure this does much for the case file.

CAROLINE

ORIGAMI YODA AND THE MIRACLE CURE

BY CAROLINE

Dear School Board Members,

I am a student at Tippett Academy now, but last year I was at McQuarrie Middle and had the wonderful privilege of meeting Dwight Tharp and becoming best friends with him.

He helped me deal with a bully problem then, and he has helped me deal with a very different problem this year at my new school.

There's a lot of "Understanding Our Differences" at my new school. That would be fine, but since I'm the one who's different, it's a big pain in my butt.

THAT WOULD BE TOTAL-LY USEFUL!

See, I have a severe hearing impairment. My audiologist calls it "profoundly deaf." But that is a little different from being completely deaf. I can hear a lot of stuff with my hearing aids, and I can read lips like a ninja. (I don't mean that ninjas read lips; I just mean that I'm that fast and that good at it.)

Anyway, I can get along just fine without any special treatment. And I didn't get any at McQuarrie. People were used to me, and nobody made a big deal about it.

But at Tippett Academy, EVERYBODY made a big deal about it.

Everybody was so busy trying to show that they "understood my differences" that I never got a chance to be normal.

And some of them had taken a sign language class, so they kept signing at me. People, I don't even know sign language! I kept telling them that I read lips and they kept waving their fingers at me.

Worst of all, some of them were practically fighting over who was going to be my friend. Mostly just to show everybody else that they were friends with someone "different."

Well, I got sick of it quick, and I told Dwight about it when I called him that night. (In case you're wondering, I can talk on the phone if it has a volume setting I can turn up. I still have trouble understanding some people, but I can understand Dwight pretty good.)

DWIGHT: Why don't you ask Origami Yoda?
ME: Come on, Dwight, just tell me what to do. You don't have to do the Origami Yoda thing for me.
DWIGHT: But I don't know what you should do. However, I think Origami Yoda does.
ME: Are you joking?
DWIGHT: No. You really need to ask Origami Yoda.
ME: Over the phone?
DWIGHT: I don't think that would work. He needs to talk to you in person.
ME: All right. Can you get your mom to drive you over to Wendy's? I could meet you there.

We meet at Wendy's every once in a while, since we don't see each other at school. My dad calls these dates. But they're not. Not exactly.

Anyway, at Wendy's, Dwight gets the kids' meal and I get a Frosty and a salad.

As soon as we sit down, Origami Yoda says, "A miracle cure you had, tell them you should."

"But there is no miracle cure," I said. "My audiologist says—"

"A cure you need not," interrupted Origami Yoda. "Tell them just."

"Wait, does he mean I should just tell them I'm cured?"

"Yeah, I think so," Dwight said from under the table. "Have you seen this periscope? This is the coolest kids' meal toy ever. I can see you!"

Then he held up Origami Yoda again.

"Band-Aids you will need."

When I got to school on Monday, the first person I ran into was Willow.

"HI, CARE-O-LINE!" she shouted at me.

"You don't have to shout anymore," I told her. "My surgery was a total success."

I pointed to the two Band-Aids on my forehead.

"WHAT?" she asked.

"Shh! That hurts my ears," I said. "My hearing is way above average now."

"Really?" she said.

REALLY??

It was so much easier for me to read her lips when she wasn't shouting and talking in drawn-out syllables.

"Yeah, I'm not deaf anymore."

"But you're still wearing your hearing aids." She said this sort of hopefully. Like she was hoping I was still a little bit "different" so she could still "understand" me.

"My doctor says I need to leave them in for a while or my ears will grow back funny," I told her.

This made no sense, of course, but neither did shouting at me, and she had been doing that for three weeks.

After a week, I took off the Band-Aids and that was that. I was still a little bit "different," but not "different" enough to fuss over.

Some people, like Willow, stopped bugging me so much, but a couple of them—Naomi and Emily—turned out to be actual friends. I hadn't even realized that before.

True, I don't always understand everything people say, but now I know who's actually worth listening to and who I can just pretend I'm paying attention to.

So, as you can see, Dwight and Origami Yoda really do help people. And if you kick Dwight out of school, he won't be able to do that anymore. He is an awesome guy.

Jeez, can you imagine being out in public and having Dwight wave that thing around while doing the world's worst Yoda impression? Now, that is embarrassing!

My Comment: First of all, you're just as embarrassing with your Darth Paper as he is with Yoda. The fact that you do the voice better is actually more embarrassing.

Second of all, you once again missed the whole point of the story!

ANOTHER HOT
DATE WITH DWIGHT!

QUAVONDO

ORIGAMI YODA AND NOTHING

BY QUAVONDO

Dear School Board,

My story about Origami Yoda starts with Mr. Good Clean Fun and his monkey.

I think it's funny that when a kid has a puppet, you want to send him to CREF. But when an adult has a puppet, you keep hiring him to come give us presentations about washing our hands and stuff.

Actually, this time Mr. Good Clean Fun wasn't there to talk about good hygiene as usual; he came to get us all excited about the school fund-raiser.

It's time for MMS'
POPCORN FUNDRAISER!

PRISES!

PRIZES!

PRIZES!

FUN!

FUN!

FUN!

Get Ready For Some GOOD CLEAN FUN!!!
Mr. GoodCleanFun and his monkey are coming
back to get us PUMPED UP about selling
collectible POPCORN tins to support our SCHOOL!
Where: Cafeteria   When: Monday, 2nd Period
Note: Attendance is mandatory.

"I wonder what kind of crap we're going to have to sell this year," I whispered to Cassie as we went into the gym for the assembly. Unfortunately, Mr. Howell overheard me. He was my teacher last year and always hated me.

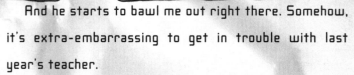

"Well, you're not going to sell anything with that attitude," he said. "Please step over here, young man."

And he starts to bawl me out right there. Somehow, it's extra-embarrassing to get in trouble with last year's teacher.

"Do you even know why our school has this fund-raiser? The money goes to fund the elective classes, since the state cut funding for 'nonessential education.' Do you understand?"

I said yes, but I guess he could tell I had no idea what he was talking about.

"What elective are you in?"

"I don't know," I said. "Democrat?"

"NO! I'm talking about your elective class! Like band or art."

"Oh, I'm taking Mr. Randall's LEGO robots class."

Howell rolled his terrible yellow eyes.

"Well, it's going to be pretty hard for you to build a LEGO robot without any LEGOs. That's what you kids

MR. GOOD CLEAN FUN!

SOAPY THE MONKEY

don't understand. You see, the money for those classes has to come from somewhere and . . ."

Thankfully, Mr. Good Clean Fun and Soapy the Monkey came out onstage then and Mr. Howell let me sit down.

They showed us these mini-cans of popcorn we were supposed to sell. Each mini-can was a collector's tin, he told us. One had pictures of a cottage in a snowstorm painted by somebody famous. Or we could sell a can with any team's football helmet on it. Or motorcycles, kittens, or Native Americans. And the popcorn came in different flavors.

$10

$23

IT'S FUN!

They passed out these Edu-Fun Popcorn Products catalogs that had all the different cans in them. I was, like, WHAT? Ten bucks a can? How are we supposed to sell popcorn in an ugly can for $10? And I knew there was no way in the world I was going to sell any regular-size cans, which were $23!

Then we heard about all these pizza parties the top classes would win, and Mr. Good Clean Fun showed us a big jar of dollar coins and said the person who sold the most cans could scoop out a whole handful. Gee, maybe they'd get a whole $10 and could buy themselves another can of popcorn.

WHEE!

YEP!

I noticed that Mr. Good Clean Fun didn't actually open any of the cans of popcorn and let us taste it. Probably because he knew we would have puked.

So when I got to LEGO robots class, I asked Mr. Randall if it was really true that we needed to sell popcorn to pay for LEGO stuff.

He had a long explanation about the school's electives fund, but basically he said "yes." He looked like he was embarrassed for us to have to go out and sell those dumb cans.

MR. RANDALL

"Remember how you guys asked if we were going to go to the regional FIRST LEGO League competition? And I said we'd have to wait and see?"

"Yeah."

"Well, this is what we were waiting to see: how much money would be in the fund after the fund-raiser."

"Ugh," I said.

So at lunch I went to see Dwight. He's always moping around these days because of his girlfriend not being here, but Origami Yoda seems as Jedi wise as ever.

"Origami Yoda, how are we supposed to sell all that popcorn?" I asked Dwight, who was pushing a roll around in a pool of gravy with one hand and holding up Origami Yoda with the other.

"Too late," said Kellen. "We already asked."

"Well, what did he say?"

"Nothing you must sell," said Origami Yoda, Kellen, and Tommy at the same time.

"But we have to sell it," I told Origami Yoda. "Apparently, that's the only way we're going to get to take our robot to the FLLs."

"Yeah," said Kellen. "Ms. Richards told us the same thing in art class. We need to sell the junk to pay for art supplies."

"But how?" I asked.

"Nothing you must sell," repeated Origami Yoda.

"Yeah, we've heard, Dwight—now can it," hollered Harvey from the end of the table. "Your dumb advice is even dumber than usual. Don't make me get out Darth Paper to shut you up."

Then Kellen and Tommy started yelling at Harvey. They're all fighting all the time these days.

But I started thinking . . . maybe Origami Yoda was actually telling us something useful. I mean, he always does.

"You don't want me to sell anything?"

Yoda shook his head back and forth. "No. Nothing you must sell."

"Good grief," said Harvey, and started to pull Darth Paper out of his bag. I went off to see if there was a seat at Murky's table. I just can't stand listening to Harvey anymore.

After school, I went back to see Mr. Randall before my bus came.

"If I sell a ten-dollar mini-can of popcorn, how much money actually goes into the fund?"

"Well, not ten dollars—I know that," said Mr. Randall. "There's the cost of the popcorn and the can . . ."

"And the ugly painting on the can," I added. "And they have to pay Mr. Good Clean Fun."

"And his monkey," said Mr. Randall with a funny smile. "Actually," he said, "I've heard that the school only keeps half the money. But don't quote me on that."

"So, say I talk my grandmother into supporting the school by buying an outrageously overpriced mini-tin of popcorn she doesn't even want. What does the school get? Five bucks?"

"I guess so."

"What if I just sold her nothing for five dollars?"

Q'S GRANDMOTHER →

NOTHING! ONLY $5! [ ] BUY NONE GET NONE FREE!

"Nothing?"

"Yeah, it would be cheaper than the ten dollars and it wouldn't clutter up her house and it wouldn't be ugly, but I would get the same amount of money for the school."

Mr. Randall smiled.

"Quavondo, that's not a bad idea at all."

"Thanks, but it wasn't mine. It was Origami Yoda's."

What really surprised me was how many people bought more than one nothing.

My grandmother, for example, bought five. That's $25 worth of nothing.

"Q, I've got twelve grandkids—you're my favorite, of course—and each year each one of them calls me up to buy some kind of *$^# in a collectible can. Who collects &*%##$ cans? But I always buy, even though I know that most of that money is just going to go right back to the idiots that made the &@^$ can in the first place. So, thank you for not making me buy a can."

Then she put my granddad on the phone, and he liked the idea so much he gave me $25 too. That's $50 from one phone call. There's no way they would have bought

$50 worth of popcorn, and even if they had, that would have only been $25 for the school.

When I told my neighbors and my mom's friends that they could either buy a $10 can or just give the school $5, they all gave me at least $5. And nobody even looked at the popcorn catalog. Plus they all laughed about it, instead of grumbling about it like they did last year.

Grand total: $135. I would have had to sell $270 worth of popcorn to get that much, and I never would have been able to sell all that. Plus, if I had, I would have had to deliver it. And then everybody who actually ate it would have blamed me for getting ripped off.

I told the other kids what I was doing, and some of them tried it too. Everybody in LEGO class did, and we made a lot of money. I thought we should just keep it all for going to the competition, but Mr. Randall said we should put it in the electives fund for everybody.

Of course, when Mr. Good Clean Fun came back and handed out prizes, we didn't get anything because we hadn't sold any Edu-Fun products. But when we got to Mr. Randall's class later, he had ordered pizzas for us with his own money.

NO PRIZES FOR YOU SUCKER!

PIZZA
PIZZA
PIZZA
PIZZA

So, we actually got something for nothing!

Harvey's Comment

OK, let's not confuse the issue. Yes, the popcorn cans were stupid. Yes, it was a great idea to sell "nothing" instead. But was that idea really Paperwad Yoda's? I think not. Paperwad Yoda was just babbling. It was Quavondo's idea. That's a classic tactic of fake psychics: Throw out something vague and let the sucker think it meant something.

My Comment: ARRRGH! I can't stand the way Harvey twists everything around!

Harvey is still hung up on whether Origami Yoda is a hoax. The important thing now is to show that he is a benefit to the school. In this story, he got a bunch of kids who didn't want to sell anything to sell nothing, and we made a lot more money than we would have. The school board should be giving him a reward. Period.

He deserves a reward for this next story too . . .

CASSIE

ORIGAMI YODA AND THE BODY ODOR IN WONDERLAND

BY CASSIE

Dear School Board,

You want to hear about something great Dwight and Origami Yoda have done?

Well, we had this situation in the drama club that was getting totally ugly, and it was about to get way uglier.

See, we were doing *Alice in Wonderland: The Musical*, and there are a lot of parts, so some people who hadn't been in plays before ended up getting roles. I was the White Rabbit, by the way.

So the play was going fine and all, but the problem

LISA was Lisa, who was the Cheshire Cat. She had never been in drama club before and none of us knew her real well.

At first we didn't really realize who it was that smelled so bad. But pretty soon we realized it was Lisa. I mean, she smelled terrible.

And the thing is, we spend a lot of time very close to each other. There's no real backstage, you know, just this closet-size area on each side of the stage. And sometimes we all have to stand back there waiting for our cues, like right before the big song, "Tea Party Boogie."

And then there are times when we all sit in a circle to read through the script or whatever. And there's no way you can concentrate on remembering the words when your nose is on fire from a terrible smell.

Everybody was always trying to sit away from her, and it was getting REAL obvious.

My friend Amy, who was Tweedledum, and I whispered to each other about it. But some of the other girls started saying stuff that I was afraid Lisa would overhear. And Haley, who was Alice, actually talked to

I CANNOT CONCENTRATE BECAUSE MY NOSE IS ON FIRE.

our drama club teacher, Mrs. Hardaway, but she said we needed to accept people's differences.

Well, I was willing to try, but some of the others weren't. Then Lisa was absent one day, and that's when things got really nasty.

Brianna goes, "OMG, it is so nice to have some fresh air."

And Haley goes, "I know. We won't have to hold our breath through the whole 'Curiouser and Curiouser' dance for once."

"What I don't understand," goes Gemini, the Red Queen, "is how she can possibly smell so bad. I mean, my brother goes a week without taking a bath and he doesn't smell THAT bad."

And then people started describing what she smelled like, and it got really, really nasty.

Harvey got out his Darth Paper and said, "Offensive. Most offensive."

I think I was the only one who got his *Star Wars* reference, but I wasn't about to laugh.

Harvey, who plays the King, is, like, the world's worst actor, by the way, but since there are only two boys in drama club, he always gets a part. Mike is the other boy. He's the Mad Hatter. He's not a great actor either, but at least he's nice.

"All right, guys, stop," goes Mike. "It's not that bad."

"Yes, it is that bad," goes Darth Paper. "I find her lack of baths . . . disturbing."

"Now you're just being mean," said Amy.

"You know what I think is mean?" goes Haley. "I think it's mean of her to stink up our play. If she wants to be a pig, she should do it somewhere else."

Mike stomped off. I wish I had stomped off too, but I was sort of stuck there like a zombie. I mean, honestly, the smell bothered me a lot. I didn't want to hurt her feelings, but I did want to find a way to change the situation.

"I can't believe we've got three more weeks of rehearsals to go," said Brianna.

"We've got to do something," said Haley. "Hardaway won't do anything, so if WE don't do something, we're going to have to smell her for three weeks. No way."

"What can we do? Attack her with Febreze?" said Gemini.

"The power of Febreze is nothing compared to the power of her stink," said Darth Paper.

This time Haley and Brianna laughed, but I don't think they even knew where the quote came from.

"Shut up, Harvey," I said. "Mike's right. You guys are being too mean! What if one of us just talked to her nicely?"

"I'm not doing it," said Haley. "I don't want to get that close to her."

"Would you stop it?" said Amy. "If we do anything, we need to do it super-nice. We have to be totally careful about what we say."

"Fine," said Haley. "You guys go tell her something nice, but if you don't get her to either hose down or drop out, then I'm getting out the Febreze."

Mrs. Hardaway called us to rehearse "This Is My Wonderland," which neither me or Amy are in. So we talked about it. Neither of us wanted to say anything to Lisa, but we knew one of us had to, or Haley would do it for us.

After rehearsal, we asked Mike if he would do it.

"What would I say to her?" he asked. "I would have no idea what to say."

Then he got his big idea.

"Why not get Origami Yoda to tell her? He always knows what to say."

"Yeah, right," Harvey said. "I'm sure she'll take it better if it comes from a total weirdo with a green finger puppet."

"Nobody asked you, Harvey," I said. "Besides, unlike your obnoxious puppet, Origami Yoda does know what he's doing. He saved my butt big-time last year!"

"Mine too," said Mike.

"Yeah, I know all about your pathetic problems," said Harvey. "Let me know when you're ready for Vader to help."

"Yeah, right."

I ride the bus with Dwight, but I wanted to keep this conversation private. I asked him if Amy and I could talk to him and Origami Yoda the next day before school. He said, "Indubitably." I guessed that meant yes.

The next day, we found him in the library, on the floor in front of the encyclopedias, pounding on a tube of ChapStick with the A–Argentina volume.

"Hey, Dwight, did you bring Origami Yoda?" I asked.

He didn't say anything, but he pulled Origami Yoda out of his pocket and put it on his finger. "Hmm?"

he said in his ridiculous Yoda voice. Suddenly, asking him for advice seemed 100 percent ridiculous. If he hadn't helped me so much last year, I wouldn't have bothered.

"Do you know that girl Lisa?" Amy asked. "She's in our play and she stinks."

"So do most of the actors in the drama club," said Dwight in his regular voice.

"No, not like that," I said. "She means that Lisa smells bad."

"What so?" asked Dwight in the Yoda voice again.

"Well, it's a problem, and some of the other kids are getting nasty about it. She really needs to do something— maybe drop out of the play."

"What these kids are named?" asked Yoda.

"Brianna, Harvey, Haley, and—"

"Haley?" croaked Yoda. "Sith!"

"Yeah, she sort of is," said Amy. "That's why we want you—or actually Origami Yoda—to talk to Lisa before Haley does."

"OK," Dwight said, and he got up and left before we realized he was going. He walked straight out of the library. About ten minutes later he walked back in.

"Did you go see Lisa?"

"Yes."

"What did Origami Yoda tell her?"

"He didn't tell her anything."

"Why not?"

"He just wanted to see her hair."

"Her hair? Isn't it just normal hair?"

"I thought so," said Dwight.

"Well, when is he going to talk to her?"

"I don't know," said Dwight. "First he wants to investigate."

"Oh, no," I said. "Are you going to do that Sherlock Holmes accent again?"

"Yes, I am," said Dwight in his Sherlock Holmes accent.

"What are you going to investigate?" Amy asked.

"Yoda hasn't told me yet."

"Forget it," I said. "This is getting stupid. Are you going to help or not? Because if you're just going to make funny voices and fool around, we need to know now so we can do something else."

"Help Lisa I will," said Yoda, and then Dwight put him in his pocket and said, "The game's afoot."

Then he started banging on the ChapStick with the A–Argentina volume again.

That afternoon we had play practice again. And Lisa was there, and so was the smell. Haley was furious.

"I thought you were going to do something about the stink!" she hissed, loud enough that Lisa might have heard.

"Shh! Just chill out. Dwight's working on it."

"Dwight does not concern me, Admiral. We want that ship, not excuses," said Harvey/Darth Paper.

"Just give us some time."

"Don't fail me again," said Darth Paper.

"Oh, shut up."

The next morning we found Dwight in the library again. This time he was happy to see us.

"Look at this!" he shouted. He held up the ChapStick tube. It looked like he had yanked it apart and almost gotten it back together again. The thing you turn was sticking way out of it on a little stick.

He put his thumb on the turny thing and pushed it sort of like a syringe. The cap popped off the ChapStick and hit Amy in the eye.

PUSH HARD

CHAPSTICK

CHAPSTICK

"Wow, it works a lot better than I thought," said Dwight.

"Terrific," Amy said, feeling her eye socket for damage.

"Listen, Dwight," I said. "Did you do whatever it was Origami Yoda wanted?"

"Yes. I went last night on my bike," he said, using his Sherlock Holmes accent again. As if Sherlock Holmes used to ride down Route 24 on a bike.

"Where did you go?"

"To Ryland Estates."

"Isn't that the trailer park behind where Walmart used to be?"

"Yes."

"Let me guess," I said. "That's where Lisa lives?"

"Elementary, my d—"

I cut him off. "So you went to her house?"

"No."

"Where did you go?"

"The Ryland Estates laundry building."

"And?"

"They don't have one."

"So?"

"Watch this," said Dwight, and he held up the ChapStick again.

I grabbed it out of his hand.

"Would you stop being a dipwad and tell us what's going on?"

"OK," said Dwight. And all of a sudden, he was completely normal. Like a totally different person. It was kind of scary.

NORMAL?

"Don't you see," he said, without any fake British accent. "Lisa's not dirty. Her hair is perfectly clean. It's her clothes that are dirty. She doesn't have a washer and dryer in her house. So they have to drive somewhere to do their laundry at a Laundromat, and for whatever reason her parents don't have the time or the money to do that right now. That part's none of our business, really, but I'm sure there's no happy reason for it."

"Jeez," I said. I hadn't really thought about why someone might smell bad.

"What are we going to do about all that?" said Amy. "It's still going to hurt her feelings whether we tell her that she stinks or that her clothes stink."

"Why don't you ask Origami Yoda?" said Dwight.

"Again? Are you kidding? He hasn't gotten us anywhere," I said.

But Amy goes, "OK, Origami Yoda, what do we do?"

Dwight held up Origami Yoda and croaked, "Dress rehearsals you must start."

"But the play is three weeks away!" I said.

"Dress rehearsals you must start!"

"But—"

"DRESS REHEARSALS YOU MUST START!!!"

"But—"

"MUST!"

So we did.

For three weeks, we each got into our costumes every day after school, and every single one of us smelled the same—like costumes that had been in an old, slightly damp cardboard box for a couple of years.

But the important thing is that nobody ever said anything to Lisa, and her feelings never got hurt. And the play was great!

And I think that's proof that even though Dwight is a little weird, he is a good guy to have at Ralph McQuarrie Middle.

Harvey's Comment

This was Yoda's worst solution of all time! Do you know how hot that King costume was? Every day after school for three weeks I had to wear that thing and march around.

Also, I can see that this case file is really all about making me seem like a villain. ok, fine, I'm the bad guy because I made a couple of jokes privately, without Lisa even hearing them.

I guess nobody thinks Dwight might be a bad guy for ALMOST SHOOTING A GIRL'S EYE OUT!!!

My Comment: Yeah, I think the ChapStick Rocket ended up on Rabbski's list of "unacceptable behaviors." I'm pretty sure Dwight ended up in ISS for it.

But this story shows that when something important is on the line, Dwight is actually a lot more kind and considerate than some of the "normal" kids at school.

HARVEY THE KING*

*OF BAD ACTING!

THE PRE-EATEN WIENER

ORIGAMI YODA AND THE PRE-EATEN WIENER

BY MIKE

Dear School Board,

Having had some time to reflect on the incident with the pre-eaten wiener, I have come to the conclusion that Dwight/Yoda are the good guys while the rest of the kids around here are a pack of wild savages who would think it was really funny if I ended up puking from food poisoning or getting a tapeworm or worse!

What happened was, one day at lunch I got a hot dog that had a bite out of it already. Or at least it looked like it did. Maybe it was just a mutant hot dog. Either way, it's proof that this school system does not take food quality seriously.

Note: In no way do I blame our lunch ladies or Lunch Man Jeff. There is no way they would have served this freaky wiener if they had seen it first. They can only serve what you, the school board, buy. And you guys buy junk.

Anyway, I got the wiener. It was repulsive.

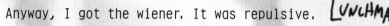

"I'll give you a dollar if you eat it," said Tommy.

You can already see the crass, careless attitude of my fellow students. Probably they have watched so many reality TV shows that they think people will do anything for money.

"Yeah, I'll give you a dollar too," said Kellen.

Well, two dollars was enough to make me think about it. Maybe it had just been caught in a machine at the hot dog plant. Maybe it hadn't really been eaten by somebody. But then I thought that maybe the "somebody" was a "something." Yuck.

"Eat it! Eat it!" Tommy and Kellen started chanting, and it took two seconds for the rest of the table to start too. And then everybody was looking at us. And Kellen was holding up the wiener for people to see.

Principal Rabbski started walking toward us from the other end of the cafeteria.

"Here comes Rabbski! Better do it fast!" said Tommy.

Harvey held up his Darth Vader puppet.

"There will be a substantial reward," it boomed. "I'll make it three dollars."

"Eat it! Eat it!"

I was about to do it when suddenly a squeaky voice squawked in my ear, "Eat it do not!"

It was Origami Yoda. Dwight had come over to my seat so Yoda could sniff the hot dog.

"Smells like rat saliva. Vomiting and diarrhea you seek, hmm?"

"No," I said.

"Then Lunch Man Jeff, a new hot dog give you he will."

Principal Rabbski showed up and started fussing at Dwight.

"Every time there's a problem, I find you right in the middle of it. I've just about had it. Oh, and, of course, you've got that puppet. For the millionth time, would you put that thing away! Now, will you please tell me what is going on here?"

"Purple," said Dwight.

Rabbski actually growled. She grabbed Dwight by the arm and hauled him off to the office.

"I can't believe you guys were trying to make me eat that," I said when she left.

"I can't believe you're not going to," said Harvey. "Rabbski's gone now."

"Didn't you hear what Origami Yoda said? He smelled rat saliva."

"Uh," said Harvey, "I'd like to remind you that not only is Paperwad Yoda not real, even if he was real, HE DOESN'T HAVE A NOSE!"

"Oh," I said. "Yeah, well, I'm still not eating it."

"You're passing up three bucks because of Paperwad Yoda? You're an idiot!"

"OK," I said, "then you eat it, Harvey. I'll give you three dollars myself."

Tommy and Kellen both said they'd add a dollar each.

"Five dollars," said Kellen. "Plus a chance to prove that Origami Yoda is wrong!"

"No problem," said Harvey, and he ate the hot dog. Then he held up Darth Paper:

"All too easy."

We gave him the five bucks.

He threw up in math class.

Harvey's Comment

I still don't think there was anything wrong with that hot dog. I think the problem was that Mike and Kellen had been waving it around and got their germs all over it.

My Comment: That was totally worth a dollar!

TOMMY
SARLACC

✳ THE ABSENCE OF ORIGAMI YODA AND THE SERIES OF DISASTERS RESULTING FROM IT

BY TOMMY

Dear School Board,

So you've already heard about how Dwight got sent home after the whole "Prepare to meet your Doom" thing. Well, here's what happened right after it: DOOM!

It was like the minute Dwight and Yoda were gone, everything they had helped us achieve did a nosedive into the sarlacc pit. And it feels like we're still in there getting slowly digested.

Despite all that home ec pizza bagel stuff, Amy and Lance got in this huge argument about a book and aren't speaking to each other now.

Could Origami Yoda have prevented that? Totally: "Lance, spoil ending of *Holes* you must not."

Then Mike ended up bawling in class again. For reasons no one knows, he brought in a bunch of his Warhammer figures. This kid, Chad, thought they were action figures and picked one up and broke it. Mike went nuts. He was crying and accusing everybody, like there was some sort of conspiracy to break his Warhammer figures. Could Origami Yoda have prevented that? Totally: "Bring breakable toys to school do not."

Could Yoda have helped me too? I sure wish he had. Because my life sucks right now, all because I bought Sara the wrong thing.

You already read about Lance and Amy and the pizza bagels. Well, that's what Sara has been doing with Tater Tot. Sitting with him in home ec, every single day! It makes me sick to think about it.

I don't have any classes with her, so I'm lucky if I get to talk to her for a couple of minutes before school or at lunch. Meanwhile, he's there with her, cooking and goofing around in the kitchen like some kind of cable TV romance movie.

But I had a chance to make up for all that by buying her an awesome birthday present.

If Origami Yoda had been around, I would have asked him what to get her. Of course, I e-mailed Dwight to see if he would ask Origami Yoda and e-mail me back. But he never answered.

But I wasn't too worried, because I had a great idea and got her this amazing graphic novel, *Robot Dreams*. It's so great. It's this really beautiful story, and I thought she would go crazy for it.

I gave it to her in the library before school. She kind of looked at it funny, like

she wasn't sure about it. But I knew once she started reading it she would love it.

And then guess who shows up? Tater Tot! With a teddy bear! Dressed like Elvis! You squeeze its foot and it plays Elvis singing "Teddy Bear."

Even then I didn't realize what a total disaster it was until the next day when Rhondella told Mike, who told me, that Sara was going on a date with Tater Tot. They were going out to play miniature golf together. That made me feel sicker than the pizza bagels.

And all because he was the one who bought her a teddy bear while I got her a book. ARRGGGHHH!!! If only Origami Yoda had been here to say, "Teddy bear you must buy." I could have at least found one that was less obnoxious than Tater Tot's.

But things are even worse for Kellen.

Sara still likes me as a friend, I guess. I hope.

But Rhondella HATES Kellen now. She won't even talk to him after what he did.

Origami Yoda could have told him, "NO! DO IT NOT! DO IT NOT!" and he would have listened, because Kellen always does whatever Origami Yoda says.

But Origami Yoda wasn't there to say no and Kellen never listens to me, so he did it and now Rhondella wants to kill him.

Harvey's Comment

The problem with you guys is you blame me or Darth Paper or Dwight being gone for everything. I mean, Kellen shouldn't need Jedi wisdom to know that his artwork makes people want to barf. Anyone with a brain would have known that Rhondella would freak.

My Comment: Yeah, "freak" is a good word for it.

Kellen's comment:

NO COMMENT!

BOO-HOO TEARS

THE ABSENCE OF ORIGAMI YODA AND THE PRINCESS RHONDELLA

BY RHONDELLA

I don't even know why I need to write about this, Tommy. Just show them that picture! That's all you need to do.

I spend a whole weekend making perfectly normal posters that say

VOTE FOR RHONDELLA
★★★★★
RHONDELLA FOR VICE PRESIDENT
★★★★★
A STUDENT COUNCIL LEADER YOU CAN DEPEND ON.

Blah. Blah. Blah.

I come in to school to put them up, and the halls are plastered with a million copies of THAT PICTURE!

If Kellen needs a finger puppet to tell him not to do something that stupid, then what he really needs is a psychiatrist!

I tried to take them all down, but I think my opponent, Brianna, must have gotten one and made copies and put them back up.

It's no wonder I lost!

So, yeah, if Origami Yoda can keep Kellen from doing stuff like this, then BRING BACK DWIGHT . . . PLEASE!

MAKE A PRINCESS YOUR VICE-PRESIDENT

YOU'RE MY ONLY HOPE!

VOTE FOR PRINCESS RHONDEL-ZEIA!

THAT PICTURE

THE REST OF
THE STORY

BY TOMMY AND KELLEN

So that's the end of the case file that I'm going to show to the school board later this week. I don't know if it's going to do any good, but that's what we've got.

You may be wondering why I let Harvey comment on the case file—after all, he's been waving Darth Paper around and making a jerk of himself all year. Kellen had been trying to get me to kick him off our lunch table. I was, like, "How am I supposed to do that? He just sits there. I never invited him."

So that's why he was still sitting with us. And when he found out that Kellen and I had finished the case file, he said, "OK, let me see it and I'll make my comments."

"Why should he let you make comments?" Kellen asked. "You're just going to say the same stuff anyway: 'Paperwad this. Paperwad that. Blah, blah, blah.'"

"Are you guys afraid of what I'm going to say? Are you afraid I'll poke holes in your little theories about Dwight using the Force?"

"No," I said. "That's not even what this case file is about. It's about whether Dwight—"

"Yeah, yeah, yeah. You talk about making a case file, but if you're afraid to include someone's opinions or other ideas, then it's not really a case file. If you want it to be scientific, you have to let other people look at it and critique it."

"But the school board—"

"Fine, if you don't want to show my comments

to the school board, you don't have to. But I think they belong in the case file. They might even help you. They're certainly more useful than Kellen's awful drawings."

"You haven't even seen the drawings, so how do you know they're awful?" snapped Kellen.

"You're right," said Harvey. "It is unfair for me to criticize either the drawings or the files without seeing them. That's why I just want to take a look."

"OK," I said, "you can look at it for a couple of minutes. But don't write any comments on it!"

"No problem," said Harvey, and he held out his hand for it.

I pulled the case file out of my backpack and handed it to him.

As he grabbed it with one hand, he held up Darth Paper with the other.

"I HAVE YOU NOW!" Darth Paper shouted, and Harvey jumped up and took off out of the cafeteria and down the hall with the case file.

I looked at Kellen.

"What's his deal?" I asked.

"Dude, I think you have just underestimated the power of the Dark Side."

He was right. I had.

We tried to chase him, but of course we got yelled at by Mr. Howell, who has Kellen-radar or something. Then the bell rang for fifth period.

We caught Harvey in the library after class.

"Give us the case file, Harvey!"

"Sure," he said calmly, and handed it to me.

I flipped through it. Not only had he crumpled it all up, he had already written his nasty Dark Side comments all over it!

"You know, I'm a very fast reader," he said with that awful smirk of his. "Thank you so much for the opportunity to read this ahead of time. I was able to put some real thought into my counterarguments."

"Counterarguments?" I said.

"Yes, you'll find it all in my conclusion," he said, and flipped to the end of the case file.

He had added these pages:

Origami Yoda DoesN't Belong Here

by Harvey

Dear School Board Members,

I come to school to learn, not to watch a daily puppet show.

I support Principal Rabbski's attempts to help us focus on our schoolwork, especially the important Standards of Learning tests.

For this reason I have always objected to Dwight's use of the finger puppet, especially in the library and classroom. I also object to many of Dwight's other activities, which also interfere with the learning process but which are too numerous and too gross to list here.

When you consider the stories in the so-called case file that Tommy has collected, you'll notice that the recurring theme is Dwight disrupting the learning environment, over and over again:

- Talking a student out of taking a model rocketry class so that he could sit with a girl he likes in home ec.

- Potentially jeopardizing the school fund-raiser.
- Turning the class insect collection activity into an unpleasant game of one-upmanship.
- And, most seriously, issuing a strange and ominous statement that could easily be seen as a threat.

Now, I do not believe that Dwight would really want to hurt anyone, but as you have heard, his strange statements certainly have the power to upset people who are not so sure about his intentions.

For this reason, I encouraged Jen to tell Principal Rabbski about the "Zero Hour comes. Prepare to meet your Doom!" threat that Dwight made.

I feel that we are a big family at McQuarrie Middle School, and it's every student's job to look out for the other students. I felt it best for everyone that a responsible adult was made aware of Dwight's statement.

I hope that Dwight receives the help he needs and that everyone will eventually realize that I have acted in his best interests as well as those of McQuarrie Middle School.

Thank you for your time.

Harvey

Harvey had this proud look on his face when we finished the letter. "So it was you! You were the one who got Jen to complain about Dwight!" I shouted.

"I have to admit, I never expected that to be so effective," said Harvey with his super-evil smirk back on full blast.

I wanted to punch it right off his face!

"I can't believe you would do that!" I yelled.

"I can," said Kellen. "I've told you not to underestimate the Dark Side!"

"So," says Harvey, "are you going to show my comments to the school board?"

"Are you crazy?" I said. "You've twisted everything to make Dwight look bad. Of course I'm not going to show them to the school board!"

"Mmm-hmm," said Harvey. "I knew you would say that. That's why I copied them. I'm going to come and read them to the school board myself!"

"What?!"

I felt like that kid Jedi in *Revenge of the Sith* who's, like, "Hey, Anakin, what's up?" and then Anakin slices him with his lightsaber. I was a fool. I had given Harvey all the ammunition he needed to shoot down everything.

Harvey held up Darth Paper: "You were unwise to lower your defenses."

"Would you shut up!" I yelled. I grabbed it off his finger, crumpled it up, and threw it on the floor.

Harvey picked up the wad of paper and made it say, "Yes, release your anger. Feel the power of the Dark Side."

"Would you stop for one minute! This is serious. You're not really going to go to the school board meeting, are you? They could kick Dwight out!"

"Sure I am. You get up and read them your little files, and then I'll read them my counterarguments. We'll see who they believe."

"No, you can't do that," I said.

"Why not?" said Harvey. "It's a school board meeting. 'Every student, teacher, parent, or member of the public has a right to attend.'"

"Shove it!" I shouted.

Everybody looked at us, and Mrs. Calhoun started walking over. I picked up my stuff and took off before she could tell me to. Kellen came too.

"See you tomorrow night," called Harvey in a fake friendly voice. "The meeting's at seven, right? Save me a seat!"

"I said, shove it!" I shouted over my shoulder. That made Mrs. Calhoun follow me out of the library and give me an ISS slip. That's the first time I've ever been sent to ISS. If I'd known I was going to get in trouble, I would have said something better than "shove it."

You know, when Origami Yoda first showed up, I spent all my time wondering if he was really using the Force. But when Darth Paper showed up, I never considered it. I figured it was just Harvey being annoying and quoting movie lines.

But as I stomped off to the office, I wondered for the first time . . . could Darth Paper really be leading Harvey to the Dark Side of the Force? I mean, Harvey's been a jerk before, but this was just evil!

While I was sitting in the office doing my time, I realized that Dwight was in bigger trouble than I was then.

Origami Yoda had told me that the case file could save Dwight. But because I had let it fall into the wrong hands, it was powerless now. Harvey would counter every good point in it. At best, it would balance out. But more likely, Harvey might actually make the school board believe that Dwight really was "disrupting the learning environment."

So, basically, after a week and a half without Dwight, absolutely everything had gone wrong, and Darth Paper was set to rule the galaxy. We were in deep trouble.

There was only one hope: Origami Yoda.

I had tried e-mailing, texting, and phoning Dwight but hadn't gotten any answers except for the Rib-B-Q request. But this time I really, really had to get through to him. I decided to go to his house after school and make him listen.

EMERGENCY
YODA

ORIGAMI YODA
AND THE FIVE FOLDS

BY TOMMY

Dwight and Sara both live over on one of those little dead-end streets off of Cascade Drive. Not that far from me, really, but I had never been back there before. Other than crossing Route 24, it's a pretty easy bike ride.

I knew Sara's address because we wrote a few letters over the summer.

I passed her house first, but I didn't see her outside or anything. I was kind of glad. I didn't have any idea what I would say to her.

Dwight's house is right next to hers. I

guess I figured that since Dwight was so weird, his house would be really weird too. But it looked totally normal. I didn't see any holes in the yard. Sara says he's always sitting in holes. Those must be in the back. I did see the fence that Sara's dad had built so he wouldn't have to look at Dwight sitting in the holes.

I knocked on the door. No answer. Then I saw the doorbell, so I rang it.

Dwight's mom came to the door. I had seen her at school that one time, but I didn't actually know her.

"Hi, Mrs. Tharp, I'm Dwight's friend Tommy. I really need to talk to him."

"Oh. Tommy. Hmm. Errr. Well. See . . ."

And she tells me all this stuff about how Dwight is grounded and isn't allowed to call people or use the computer or play video games. But how she hadn't actually made a rule against people coming over. However, if she had thought that someone might, she probably would have, but since she didn't . . . and on and on.

I realized she was really talking to herself more than to me. I wanted to go, "Uh, you're the mom, just say yes or no."

Instead, I said, "This is really important, Mrs. Tharp. I really need to talk to Dwight about the school board meeting tomorrow night."

She finally let me in. The house WAS weird, but only because it was so un-weird that it was weird. It was like this beach house my family stayed in for a week one summer. You could tell that no one really lived there and that all the stuff was just there to fill up blank space, not because someone had really liked it.

"Dwight's up in his room. I'll call him down."

"Actually, Mrs. Tharp, maybe I could talk to him up there?"

• • •

You never know what Dwight is going to be like. I sort of pictured him jumping up and shaking my hand. "Hey, Tommy, I've missed you guys! Thanks for working on this case file for me!"

Instead, I got to his room and he was slouched on his bed just staring at the floor with a shoe in his hand. He looked over at me, but more like at my feet.

"Dwight!" His mother fussed. "Your friend is here. Can't you sit up and say hello?"

He said, "Hello."

It didn't exactly give me a warm, fuzzy feeling.

His room was almost empty. I thought he'd have *Star Wars* posters and action figures and all kinds of stuff. Nope. The stuff on the walls was obviously stuff his mother had put up . . . when he was in preschool. Seriously, who has a fake anchor hanging on their wall?

The only thing that was Dwight-like was the origami. There was a huge pile of it on top of his dresser. The dresser had all its drawers open and clothes hanging out.

"Oh, Dwight, I thought you were going to put those clothes away NEATLY," his mom said.

He got up—slowly—and started to move toward the dresser.

"Well, it's too late now. Don't do it now. You have a guest."

Dwight sat back down on his bed.

"Well, I'll let you boys talk," his mom said. She walked out of the room, but stood near the door looking back in for a while. Finally, she left.

Dwight came to life a little bit, but not much.

"Dwight, have you gotten any of my e-mails or anything?"

"No. When Sara brought the Rib-B-Q, Mom realized I was e-mailing people and took away my computer, my cell phone—everything."

"TV, too?" I asked, since that's my parents' favorite thing to take away.

"I wasn't allowed to watch TV to start with," he said.

No TV! That explains a lot! No wonder he never has any idea what we're talking about! "Well, listen. I've got some bad news. I need your help. Can you get out Origami Yoda?"

"My mom took him."

"Oh, man! We need him! There's big trouble! It's Harvey."

Dwight looked up at me for the first time. Then he looked at the floor again.

"I was stupid and let him read the case file. You remember the one Origami Yoda told me to make? Now Harvey's created a sort of ANTI case file. He makes you sound awful. And he's going to read it to the school board tomorrow night!"

"Huh."

"Yeah, I mean, I think you'll end up at CREF for sure. Are you listening, Dwight? You don't want to go to CREF. Seriously."

Dwight looked at his door for a minute. Then

he walked over to his dresser and pulled a piece of green origami paper out of a plastic bag.

"I'll make an emergency Yoda," he said. "This is my new five-fold method."

It took him about fifteen seconds and he had a Yoda finger puppet . . . sort of. It wasn't much more than a rectangle with two triangle ears sticking out.

"That's cool," I said. "But isn't it kind of . . . uh . . . simple?"

"Thanks," he said as he drew a face on it with a ballpoint pen. "In origami, simplicity can be more valuable than complexity. The key is choosing only the necessary details—"

"Uh, yeah, what I meant was . . . it's so simple, is it still going to be able to use the Force?"

"Judge me by the number of folds do you?" the new Origami Yoda said.

"Uh, no?" I said.

"Worried about Harvey are you?"

"Yes! It's like he's gone to the Dark Side!

He's walking around with his Darth Paper and now he's got this—"

"Worry do not," said Origami Yoda. "Make it right I will."

"This is serious. If we don't stop him, he's going to get you sent to CREF! He's being a total jerk about it. I hate him."

"No!" said Origami Yoda. "Hate to the Dark Side only leads."

"Well, then, I really, really dislike him."

"No," said Yoda. "Forgive him you must."

"Forgive him? He's getting you thrown out of school! He's just doing this to be mean."

"Difficult it is to be right when no one believes you."

"Dwight? Is that Yoda talk?" His mother had shown up at the door. "I'm sorry to do this in front of your guest, but this is going to be strike three. I can't BELIEVE you've made ANOTHER Yoda after I caught you talking to Sara with it and SPECIFICALLY told you not to make another one. Give it to me."

He handed it to her. She unfolded it.

"Sorry, but this is going in the recycling bin."

She turned to me.

"Tommy, I think you'd better go home. Thank you very much for coming to see Dwight. Hopefully, he'll be back in school soon and you'll be able to see him there." As soon as she started to say the "hopefully" part, her voice cracked a little bit. She looked like she was going to cry.

I figured it would be best if I left quickly. I wasn't going to get to talk to Origami Yoda anymore and I wasn't getting anywhere with Dwight anyway.

Forgive Harvey? No, I couldn't do that. Was Dwight crazy?

But even weirder was that thing about how being right is difficult. Surely he didn't mean that Harvey was right? Because that would mean that Origami Yoda really was phony.

Is that what he meant?

It's Friday, the day of the school board meeting. But before I go to the meeting, I'm going to go ahead and write down what happened at school today. It was huge! And bad! Hugely bad!

At lunch, Kellen and I were discussing ways of stopping Harvey. I have to admit that most of them involved one or both of us punching him.

Sara walked over with a note. For a minute I thought it was a note from her for me! Maybe she had changed her mind about Tater Tot! Maybe Origami Yoda had done it. Maybe it was an apology/love note!

But it wasn't from her, and it wasn't for me.

"I saw Dwight this morning," she said. "He threw this letter out of his window at me when I went to get on the bus. He asked me to bring it to the table here at lunch."

She gave me the envelope.

"I'm pretty curious," she said, "so if you don't mind, I want to stay and find out what it says."

This is what it said on the envelope:

Don't open yet!
Please have Harvey read this letter out loud at the lunch table. Don't read the letter without Harvey!

We figured this letter was part of Origami Yoda's plan and he must have a reason for doing it this way, so Kellen went across the cafeteria to get Harvey. I could see them arguing. Harvey was being a stubborn butt as usual. But he finally came—with Darth Paper, of course.

"You may dispense with the pleasantries, Tommy," Darth Paper said. It was a new, uncrumpled one.

"I wasn't going to use any pleasantries," I said, and gave Harvey the envelope.

He opened it up and pulled out a sheet of paper. Origami Yoda fell out and fluttered to the floor. I snatched him up. It wasn't the five-fold one. It was the real one.

Harvey started reading. "Dear Everybody, especially Harvey, Harvey is right about Origami Yoda."

"WOOOOO!" hollered Harvey. "Finally! At last! Halla-Yoda-Loo-Yaa! I told you and I told you and I told you."

"Seriously, Harvey, what does it really say?"

"That's what it really says! Look!"

He handed me the letter. He started doing a little dance.

"And you all thought I was being a jerk. But I was right the whole time!"

"Maybe, but you were also a jerk the whole time," said Sara.

Me and Kellen and everybody were all trying to read the letter at once.

Here is the whole thing:

Dear Everybody, especially Harvey,

Harvey is right about Origami Yoda.

It is just paper. A really nice piece of paper, but just paper. There is no Force. Just me talking.

Tommy, you can have Origami Yoda. My mom threatened to recycle it, too. Don't lose it. Keep it in one of your case files. Not because it's magic, just to remember all the stuff that happened.

Dwight Tharp

P.S. Thanks for the Rib-B-Q sandwich. If they have it again, please buy me one and give it to Sara again. I wonder if they will have Rib-B-Qs at CREF.

That letter was, like, the saddest thing I had ever read. I thought he was going to come up with some kind of amazing Jedi plan. Instead, he was just giving up.

Harvey stood up on his chair. He raised Darth Paper in the air over his head.

"Now I am the master!" shouted Darth Paper. "This is a day that will be long remembered!

It has seen the death of Origami Yoda, and tonight it will see the end of Dwight."

The bell rang. The crazy thing about school is that no matter what's going on when the bell rings, you have to get up and move.

So even though everything was a disaster and I had no idea what to do next and the one thing I believed in turned out to be a piece of paper and the main thing I wanted to do was knock Harvey off the chair, I just sort of moved like a burned-out droid toward my locker.

I had Origami Yoda in my hand. Just a piece of paper.

Now there was no hope that he was going to come back and make everything right again. He wasn't even real.

Then I started to wonder about the case file. Why was I making the case file? Because Origami Yoda had told me to? But if Origami Yoda wasn't real . . .

This sounds really bad, but for one tiny second I wondered why I should care if it worked. I was so mad, I thought I really didn't care anymore if Dwight got kicked out. I mean, I believed in Origami Yoda! I did all kinds of stuff because he told me to. And it was all a joke or something?

But in a weird way, it wasn't Dwight I was mad at. Plus I started to think how pathetic he must feel. Sitting at home. Getting yelled at by his mom. Worrying about CREF. And then having to bow down and write that letter to Harvey.

I knew I still wanted to help him. But I had no idea how.

Then I had a crazy idea. I put Origami Yoda on my thumb.

"What can I do?" I asked.

He didn't answer.

We were all doomed.

I was almost to my locker when I saw Principal Rabbski up ahead. She likes to stand in the middle of the hallway so that all the kids have to detour around her.

I put my hand up and pointed Origami Yoda right at her.

"If you strike down Dwight, he will grow more powerful than you can possibly imagine!" said Origami Yoda.

Rabbski sighed.

"Tommy, I think it's time you and I had a little talk."

She made me follow her into her private office. I had never been in there before. Not to change the subject, but she had a Rubik's 4x4 Cube on her desk . . . solved!

"Listen, Tommy," she started. "I've heard about your petition or whatever it is that you're going to give the school board tonight. I can't talk to you about another student's disciplinary problems, but there are a few things you need to understand."

She had a lot to say. A lot of it was about the Standards of Learning tests that we have to take and how important they are to the students and to the school. She said some students were a constant distraction from the Standards of Learning. Not only were they hurting themselves, they were also hurting other students and the whole school, since school funding was based on test scores.

"When I see you in the office for screaming at another student one day, and the next day you're walking down the hall with a Yoda puppet, being disrespectful to me, that just proves my point," she said. "You're a good kid, but another kid has got you confused and distracted. I need you to put Yoda away. Put your petition away. And concentrate on the real reason you're here: To learn. To ace the Standards test."

Well, I was confused and distracted, but there was no way I was buying all that. It had an Emperor Palpatine sound to it. You know— all that "I'm bringing peace to the galaxy" stuff he says.

"I appreciate what you're doing for your friend. I really do. But I hope you'll be able to understand that maybe what I've decided is what's best for him. OK?"

I'll never join you. Never! I thought, but I didn't say it out loud, because that seemed like a good way to end up in ISS for the rest of the day.

Now I'm home. I've propped Origami Yoda up next to my computer and he seems to be watching me carefully. It's time for me to go rescue my friend. I hope Origami Yoda thinks I'm ready.

ORIGAMI YODA AND THE SCHOOL BOARD

BY TOMMY

I just got back from the school board meeting. It was crazy. Crazeeee! I'm still not even sure what happened. Let me start at the beginning.

Neither of my parents was particularly interested in any of this—they're only particularly interested in things my brother does, but that's a whole different story—so I rode my bike to the meeting, which was held in the high school library.

The school board members were sitting at

two tables pushed together at one end of the room, and everybody else sat in chairs at the other tables.

Dwight and his mom were already there. His mom was whispering at him constantly.

Up front, Principal Rabbski was joking around with a couple of people who were maybe principals from the other schools. The school board people at their big table were whispering and laughing too. It didn't seem like a good time to be telling jokes.

Nobody else from school was there. I already knew Kellen couldn't come, and I was hoping that something would stop Harvey from coming too.

Nope. A second after I sat down at a table near Dwight's table, Harvey walked in and sat down next to me. I could have moved, but I wanted to stay near Dwight. "Have you gotten a good look at my new Darth Paper yet?" Harvey asked. It looked just like the old one to me. Dwight started to come over to our table to see it, but his mother hissed at him and he sat back down.

Some lady came around and passed out pieces of paper to everybody. They said:

Agenda

Lucas County Board of Education

October meeting

Pledge and Moment of Silence

Approval of Minutes

Public Comment

Old Business

New Business

Closed Session for Disciplinary Action—

CREF Referral Request by Lougene Rabbski

Adjourn

I guessed Dwight's thing was that "CREF Referral Request."

Harvey started snickering and whispered to me, "Can you believe her name is Lougene?"

"Shh!" I said.

A dude in a suit and tie turned on the microphone and said the meeting was about to start and everybody needed to be quiet. He was glaring at Harvey and me when he said it.

Then he told everyone to stand up and say the Pledge of Allegiance.

"Liberty and justice for all!" I said extra-loud.

Then there was a moment of silence. Then everybody on the school board voted yes about something.

Then the guy in the suit said that this was the chance for the public to speak. Members of the public had to limit their comments to five minutes.

Five minutes?! I couldn't read them the whole case file in five minutes!

Some guy got up and went to a little stand near the front tables. He talked about absolutely nothing for five minutes. And then a woman got up and said how much she agreed with him for five minutes. And then someone else said they just wanted to add a little something, and they talked for five minutes too. Now I could see why they limit people to five minutes. But I really needed more time.

"Anyone else?" the guy in the suit said.

"You first," said Harvey—with a smirk, of course.

I got up and said something. I don't know exactly what it was, but I think it was pretty good.

I told them about how so many kids at school think Dwight is a good guy. And how we all got together to write the case file. I kept holding it up to show them stuff.

And I told them about the smelly girl in the play. And the skateboard kid. And about how much money Origami Yoda's idea had made for the fund-raiser. And all that.

I told them about the disasters that happened after Dwight was gone and how much we wanted him to come back.

"Thank you very much," said the suit guy.

Was my five minutes gone already? I hoped I had said enough.

"We always love to hear from our enthusiastic students," said the suit guy. "Of course, it would be inappropriate for us to comment on a disciplinary matter in public session. But we do appreciate your concerns."

I'm not sure why, but somehow I felt like they hadn't listened to anything I had said.

But Mrs. Tharp had. When I got back to my chair, she was crying and smiling at me. She gave me a hug! I didn't know what to do.

"Oh, thank you, Tommy! I had no idea. I had no idea," she said.

I was glad she was happy, but I was afraid she was going to be crying big-time in a minute when Harvey got up and contradicted everything I had said.

"Anyone else?" said suit guy.

"Wish me luck," said Harvey.

I didn't.

But I should have.

ORIGAMI YODA
AND DOOMSDAY

BY HARVEY (AND JEN)

So I got up and started to read the school board members my speech:

"My name is Harvey Cunningham. I have come here tonight to discuss the no-games policy on school computers."

I proceeded to make a brilliant argument about the connection between video-game skills and brain development, but Tommy says I can't put that all in his case file or he'll cut it out. Anyway, the school board members just sat there like a bunch of mynocks anyway.

I realized my time was about up, so I wanted to drop my bomb about Dwight. I couldn't wait to see the look on Tommy's face.

"I would like to use the rest of my time to discuss Dwight Tharp," I told the school board members. The superintendent looked at his watch.

"I was the one who got the cheerleader to report Dwight for saying 'Zero Hour Comes. Prepare to meet your Doom!' But that was before I knew what he meant. See, I think I'm the only one who has figured it out."

The superintendent said, "Thank you, your time is up," but I acted like I didn't hear him and kept on talking. What was he going to do?

"It may interest you to know," I continued, "that the cheerleader was kicked off the cheerleading squad because of her falling grades in English. This made me wonder . . . could this be the 'Doom' that Dwight had referred to?

"I sent her a text this afternoon to ask her about it. Let me read it to you:

```
OMG! I thnk u r rite!! wasnt
threat. was warning about englsh
papr tht i blew off cuz of
cheerleading tryouts. book reprt
on r u there god its me margaret.
ddnt read it. i made sqad but got
0 on papr. that got me kckd off
sqad. that zero = my doom! dwght
ws jst tryng 2 get me 2 stdy!
```

"In case you didn't understand any of that, let me explain. Dwight's reference to Doom was a warning that Jen would lose her place on the cheerleading team. You may quibble with his choice of the word 'Doom,' but cheerleading is pretty important to Jen and—"

"Yes, thank you, young man," said the superintendent. "I think we all understood it."

"Did you?" I asked. "Did you really? Because it's important."

"Yes, thank you. You've greatly exceeded your

time limit. It's time to sit down," said the super-intendent.

I didn't sit down.

"Are this young man's parents here?" the guy asked, looking around the room. "No? Perhaps you could ask the young man to sit down, Principal Rabbski?"

Rabbski was already glaring at me and looked like she would be happy to lunge out of her seat and drag me away.

"That won't be necessary, Your Lordship," I said, and went back to my seat.

Dwight's mom gave me a big hug. Normally, I don't hug, but since she was crying and everything, I didn't complain. Dwight shook my hand. I don't like to shake hands with people, either, since they usually jam their hand into the web between my thumb and index finger and then my hand feels funny for the rest of the day. But I let Dwight do it.

Tommy looked sort of like a dead frog with its mouth hanging open. Actually, he always looks like that. But this time even more than usual!

My Comment: I may have looked like a frog, but Harvey had that awful I'm-so-great smirk of his going full blast. But I couldn't blame him. He deserved to do it this time. He really had figured out what the rest of us had missed. And it seemed like it should be enough to totally convince the school board that Dwight was OK, right?
WRONG!

"Anyone else?" asked the superintendent. "If no one else wishes to speak, we'll end the public comment period. Now, can I have a motion to go into closed session to discuss the disciplinary matter referred by Principal Rabbski?"

"I make the motion," one of the members mumbled.

"Wait just a minute!"

It was Dwight's mom.

"Uh, Mrs. Tharp, the public comment period

is now closed . . . ," the suit guy said, but I think he could tell it wasn't going to stop her.

"Why do you even need a closed meeting to vote on this?" she said, standing up. "These two students have made things pretty clear."

"I think it would be best to have this discussion in a closed meeting, Mrs. Tharp," said the suit guy.

"What is there to discuss? My son tried to warn a girl that she would lose her spot on the cheerleading squad if she got a zero—"

Principal Rabbski stood up too. "Mrs. Tharp, as I've explained to you, there is a pattern of behavior, including violence—"

"Please!" said the suit guy. "Stop right there, Ms. Rabbski. School policy does not permit discussion of CREF referrals in a public meeting!"

"But surely she's going to withdraw Dwight's CREF referral now?" went Dwight's mom. "Aren't you?"

She looked at Rabbski. Rabbski just sat back down and didn't say anything.

"You mean that after what we just heard tonight, you still want to send my child to CREF?"

Rabbski just sat there.

"We'll certainly consider what we've heard tonight," the suit guy said, "but—"

We never found out what he was going to say, because Dwight's mom went nuts.

One time Mike dragged me to one of his RightwayKidz church meetings. This wild dude was there. They called him Pastor JJ. He seemed like a nice guy until he got up and started preaching. He scared the crap out of me.

He was shouting about the end of the world and locusts with human faces and how I was going to burn in hell. And he was going nuts.

But not as nuts as Mrs. Tharp went.

"You'll consider it? YOU'LL CONSIDER IT? Well, pardon my French, but you can CONSIDER kissing my butt.

"All night long we've been hearing about a boy who has tried again and again to make friends, and God knows it isn't easy for him. But he kept on trying—reaching out in the best way he could. Until tonight I didn't know how hard he was trying—and I am so proud of him—"

Her voice started cracking. She could barely talk. And she was wiping her eyes, almost slapping the tears away.

"Really, Mrs. Tharp, I think this would be best discussed in the conference room."

"What more is there to discuss? He told a girl that she was going to get a zero on some assignment if she didn't study. So he didn't make himself clear. Well, he's got some problems putting things into words. But God forbid you should help him solve those problems, you just want to punish him for them."

"Well, Mrs. Tharp, there were other prob— er, difficulties," said Principal Rabbski, trying to get a word in. "Perhaps if we can step into the—"

"Other difficulties? It seems to me that the only difficulty is that you and your staff don't know the difference between a difficulty and a bright, creative, very special kid. Come on, Dwight, we're going home."

They started walking toward the door.

"Mrs. Tharp! We still need to come to a decision. Dwight can't return to school until—"

"Return to school?!" she shouted from the doorway. "You think I'd let him go back to your screwed-up school? We're going to find someplace where everybody doesn't have— doesn't have boogers for brains! Good night!"

AFTER
THE MEETING

BY TOMMY

They left.

Harvey said he wanted to stay to see if the school board was going to take his advice about the video games. I told him that was very, very unlikely.

Then the tie dude told us to leave so the school board could have their closed session. By the time we got outside, Dwight and his mom were long gone.

Harvey's house is pretty close. He said his dad would give me a ride home. So we started walking. I was pushing my bike, since he hadn't brought his.

"It was nice of you to try and save him," I said.

"Too bad it didn't work."

"Well, my case file didn't work either," I said.

"Yeah, well, that's because a talking piece of green paper told you to make it."

"Oh, yeah, I kind of forgot about that," I said. "It's weird, but I keep forgetting not to believe in Origami Yoda anymore."

"Yeah, that is weird. AND stupid."

"Yeah, yeah, yeah. So why did you try to save Dwight?"

"Darth Paper told me to."

"Get real."

"No, seriously. Everything that happened was part of Darth Paper's plan. Well, mostly. We weren't really trying to get Dwight kicked out. We were just trying to crack him—make him break down and admit that Origami Yoda was fake."

"And Darth Paper told you to do that?"

"Of course! He's a magic finger puppet, after all. The important thing is . . . it worked. Dwight confessed to the whole thing! At last, everybody sees that I was right all along."

"Yeah, well, everybody also thinks you're evil."

"No, I'm not," said Harvey. "I just tried to save Dwight! And you better put that in your case file! Plus look at this."

He pulled out Darth Paper. He folded the helmet up. Underneath it he had drawn a face.

"Dwight was right . . . he was right . . . ," Origami Anakin croaked. "There was some good left in me."

CONCLUSION

BY TOMMY

The next morning was Saturday. I got up around nine and checked my computer. I had an e-mail from Dwight.

Come to my house at exactly 9:45 a.m. Bring Origami Yoda!!

Underneath that was a forwarded message that the superintendent had sent his mom:

After your departure last night, the board members

voted in favor of Principal Rabbski's recommendation that Dwight be reassigned to the Correctional and Remedial Education Facility (CREF) for the remainder of the fall semester. Please contact my office to . . . BLAH BLAH BLAH.

That was hardly a surprise. We had totally blown it. Or maybe we had done a good job, but the school board just wasn't listening.

I figured that Dwight must be pretty depressed and that I should definitely go over and see him. I was pretty depressed too. And I realized it wasn't even about not having Origami Yoda around. It was about not having Dwight around. He's always been around. Since kindergarten. And I was just now realizing what a cool friend he was. Well, "cool" isn't exactly the right word. But Dwight is whatever it is he is. And life was going to be less interesting without him.

Plus I was worried that the CREF kids were going to destroy him.

But I wasn't going to tell him that. I thought maybe I could cheer him up some. He was probably sitting in a hole like a depressed zombie.

But when I got there, I saw Dwight in his front yard playing with those giant yo-yo things.

"Mom let me have my diabolos back!" he hollered, waving one of the yo-yos in the air.

He didn't seem like a zombie. He didn't even seem depressed.

"Did you bring Origami Yoda?" he asked.

"Yes, but—"

Dwight grabbed it out of my hands. He immediately put it on his finger and looked like he was having some kind of brain-wave conversation with it.

"Whew," said Dwight. "It's great to have him back. I'm probably going to need him at my new school."

I was confused—as is usual when dealing with Dwight.

"New school? You mean CREF?"

"No, my mom's decided to put me in a private school instead."

"Private school?"

"Yeah, Tippett Academy."

"Tippett Academy?! Isn't that Caroline's school?"

Dwight smiled.

And it hit me like lightning. Of course Dwight wasn't depressed! He was getting exactly what he wanted. Good-bye, Rabbski. Hello, Caroline!

I'm not one of those people who usually goes around saying OMG, but O . . . M . . . G . . . ! Once again everything had worked out exactly the way Dwight wanted. Had he been planning this all along?

If it was all some kind of crazy mad-genius plan, how far back did he start it? Just at last night's meeting? Or everything since the beginning of school?

Had the case file been part of the plan too? Was the purpose of the case file not to save him from the school board but to convince his mother that he was a good but misunderstood kid who deserved to go to Tippett instead of CREF?

If that was true, then Kellen and I—and even Harvey, I guess—had succeeded, not failed.

No, Dwight couldn't have planned all that, could he? No, I couldn't believe it. It was too much. Nobody could have figured out ahead of time how it would all work out.

Well, nobody except . . . Origami Yoda.

But Origami Yoda was fake, right? That's what the letter said.

But wait, if Origami Yoda was fake, then why did Dwight "need" him at the new school?

"Dwight, I want a straight answer."

"Yardstick," said Yoda. "Straight it is."

"No, I mean, I'm going to ask you a question and I want a straight answer. Is Origami Yoda real?"

He held up Origami Yoda: "Believe in me no more do you?"

"No! That's a question. I want a straight answer. And from you, not from Yoda."

"Yardstick."

"That wasn't funny the first time. Now, what is the answer?"

"What was the question again?"

"IS ORIGAMI YODA REAL?"

"Of course. And guess what? My mom let me have my computer back, so you can always e-mail Origami Yoda if you have questions for him to answer."

"But I thought he couldn't answer questions. I thought he was fake."

"Fake? That's mean. You're going to hurt his feelings."

"But what about that letter?"

"What letter?"

"What letter?! THE letter! The one where you told Harvey that Origami Yoda was just a piece of paper?"

Origami Yoda said: "Heard of a Jedi mind trick you have, hmm?"

A NEW HOPE

BY TOMMY

"Wait a second," I said, "do you mean—"

"Sorry," said Dwight. "I've got to go."

And he picked up his big yo-yos and practically ran back to his house.

"But if you've got to go, why did you tell me to be here right now?" I yelled after him.

"Tommy!" called someone behind me.

I turned around. It was Sara. Her family was getting into their car. She ran over to me.

"You came," she said. "Dwight's emergency Yoda said you'd come, but I just wasn't sure! I thought you were still mad at me."

"Mad?"

"About me playing miniature golf with Tater Tot."

"I wasn't mad," I said, "just—"

"Sara!" her mom hollered. "Let's go, you two."

"You're coming with us, right?" asked Sara, and she grabbed my hand and pulled me toward the car. "We're going out for brunch at Mabry Mill. You can tell me about Dwight and the school board. And I can tell you about what a jerk Tater Tot was when I beat him at Putt-Putt. And we can both talk about how awesome *Robot Dreams* is. And we can get chocolate chip pancakes."

"Chocolate chip pancakes?" I asked.

"Yeah!"

I glanced back at Dwight's house. He was looking at me from the porch and waving. I couldn't tell from that far away, but I think he had Origami Yoda on his hand.

"Sounds great!" I said to Sara.

And it was.

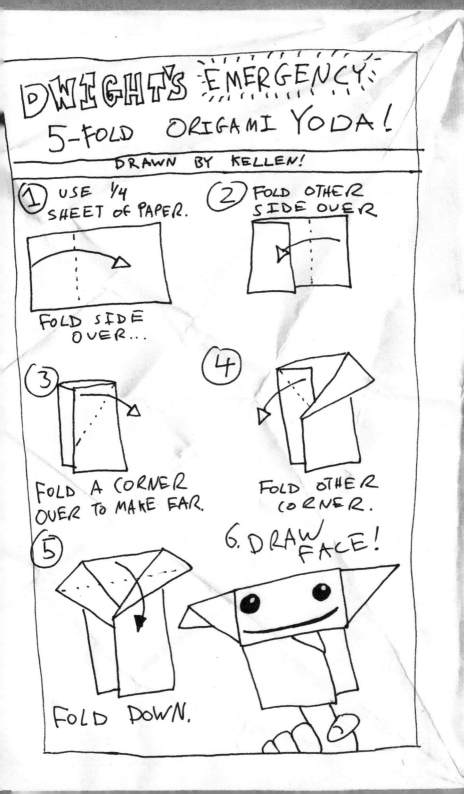

HOW TO FOLD
DARTH PAPER!!!

AS USUAL, HARVEY IS BEING A BIG
JERK AND WON'T TELL US HOW
TO FOLD DARTH PAPER....
BUT WHO NEEDS HIM?
MURKY'S FRIEND BEN →
FIGURED OUT HOW
TO CONVERT DWIGHT'S
5-FOLD YODA INTO
A 10-FOLD DARTH PAPER!

½ SHEET OF PAPER

① ② ③

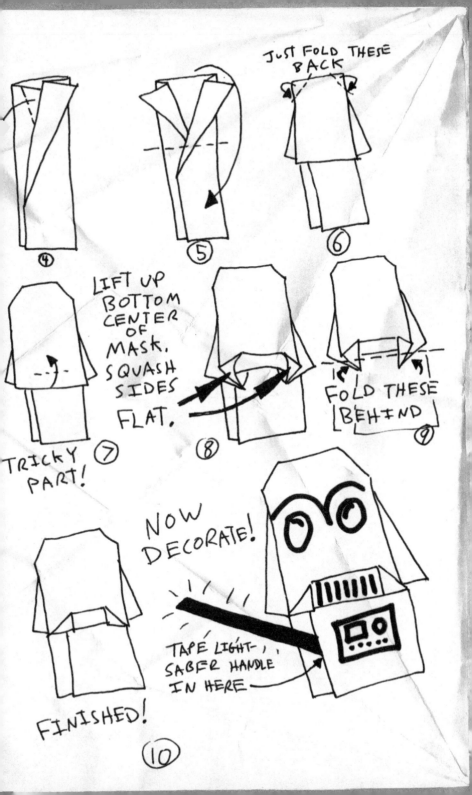

ACKNOWLEDGMENTS

I'd like to thank all the people who helped inspire, write, and produce this book ...

The Super-Folders: Oscar, Charlie, Jack, Remi, Chad and Chad, Austin, Matthew, Matt, Derek, D.T., Jordi, Sean, Tyler, Oscar H., Jessica, Jake, Mark, Connor, Cary, Houston, Jamie, Michael, Emily, Joshua, Sam, Brandy, Mr. Schell's class, Cooper, Jackson, Brennan, Carl, Chance, Jimmy, Lorenzo, Wes, the Paper Jedi Society, and everyone else who has made their own Star Wars Origami and shared it with me.

10-fold Darth Paper inventor Super-Folder Ben.

Star Wars Origami Masters: Chris Alexander, Won Park, and Fumiaki Kawahata.

George Lucas and the wonderful folks at Lucasfilm, who have made all of it possible, from making the movies in the first place to approving my ideas to just being nice.

My parents, Wayne and Mary Ann, my family,